Aloysius Tempo

Jason Johnson

Hard Solve

Verb

1. To apply whatever resources are necessary to permanently end a problem.
2. To kill.

Chapter One

Ashford, County Wicklow, Ireland

18 November 2016

08:46

I'M LOOKING at this fella from inside his own house and wondering what he would say about it all.

Would he say it's the catch, or would he say it's the cut?

I'm seeing his big bare feet slap the ground of his wide, neat garden and I'm thinking how he would respond to all this stuff going around in my head.

Would he say it's the speed or the sleep?

I'm watching his hairy B-cups jiggle as he runs a lap, attacking his heart and prolonging his life.

And my head is wondering if he would say it's the trip or the fall?

The blade or the bleed?

The gas or the gasp?

Which bit, for him, is *the* bit?

Which element of a nasty, decisive, final accident would he blame?

Would he say it's the tipping point that defines the end, or that the end stands alone?

Would he, like most, pluck out a moment, a factor, and isolate it, say it was to blame?

Would he say it's the slide or the stop, the crash or the crunch, the punch or the pavement, the germ or the disease?

Here's what I'm wondering.

I'm wondering if he knows there's never one thing that kills you.

Does he know that no one has ever accidentally died from one thing?

Does he know they were all at the end of a chain, on the edge of some steps?

Would he give a damn?

Doubt it.

Most don't.

Has he thought about stuff like that?

Probably not.

To be honest, he doesn't look like he thinks much.

He doesn't look like he knows much.

He looks like he knows very little.

He looks like a dick with tits.

I could tell him about all of this.

I could spend some time telling him how fatal accidents need components, moving parts, things that connect and detach so they can cause the damage.

Fatal accidents, I could say, need some form of weapon, some blade or drop, some wall or cord or cover or flavour that'll make a heart quit.

He's running around with the grace of an old sheep and I'm really considering explaining to him how accidents need a time frame, a space on the clock where they can turn, untroubled, from neutral to deadly.

He's plodding past this window and I could start calling out now, start saying that they need a set of circumstances, a group of factors gelling together, all part of the process, all pointing the same way.

And I could enlighten him, as he makes his way, by saying how they must arrive by surprise before they take who they have come to take.

Hello Danny Latigan, forty-nine years old.

Does he know that I am standing in his house?

Absolutely not.

There he is now, stopping, wheezing, picking his yellow Speedo out of his arse crack with two fingers.

And here am I thinking of outlining to him right now how a fatal accident is the precision instrument of bad luck.

It is the concentrated clusterfuck of misfortune.

It is the lethal friendly fire of an otherwise acceptable day.

Danny's getting into the pool and I'm thinking how I could, this moment, tell myself some things too.

I could tell myself I shouldn't be here.

I could get into explaining to my brain that I, that my own will, is things wrongly hatched in some strange sideshow, that it, like me, should be kept in some back room where they stack the incorrect.

I could tell myself some soul-sapping coldness about how I should not be here, that I was never planned, never wanted.

I could tell myself I'm an accident, that I'm error to the bone, that I'm so wrong I caused a death before I knew I was alive.

But I won't.

Christ, no.

I won't do that crap ever again.

I'm standing here looking out this big, clean window and instead, right now, I am telling myself that I have been confirmed, that I have been recognised, that I have been officially stamped and welcomed.

They want me to think like this.

They want me to be an accident, to think like an accident.

They want me to be the sort of accident you ring ahead for, the sort of problem you summon.

Right at this moment, I know everything I need to know in the world.

Because, right now, I know myself completely, and it's all fine.

And I am so very, very comfortable with that knowledge.

Right now there can never be another surprise again.

Right now I even know the future.

Right now I can predict a fact, an accident, with 100-percent certainty.

That fact is about to happen.

And here it comes.

★

'Morning Danny,' I say, and he turns as fast as he can in his heated swimming pool, eyes me through the mist lifting off the crystal blue surface of his own little mechanical lagoon.

He goes, 'Who the fuck are you?'

'Aloysius,' I say.

'This is private property.'

'No such thing anymore.'

He stands as firm as he can, stands his watery ground in those yellow Speedos, a gold chain around his throat.

A hand waves, 'Get away to fuck or I'll get the coppers.'

I walk around the pool, admiring the precise tiling, its oddly pleasing kidney shape, and Danny is watching, manning up to some kind of nuclear state.

He makes for the steps, busting to get out and get a dig at me.

'Nope,' I say. 'You're not getting out.'

'Wha?'

'You're staying in there.'

'I'm getting out now, you prick,' and he's coming for those steps.

'No,' I say, standing over them now, lifting a heavy black boot just for a second, just to show him who's the boss here. 'You're not getting out.'

'What do you want?' And he's backing away, controlling him-self in a way he's not used to doing.

'Very little.'

'Wha?'

'I want you to stay there.'

'And?'

'And nothing.'

'Someone in the house will see you and this will end badly, fella. You've no idea who . . . '

'Shut up,' I say. 'There's no one in the house.'

'There is,' he says, pointing over at it, forty feet away. We both take it in, an ivy-clad, mock-Tudor monster, with less class than whatever broken farmyard it replaced. I see his eyes flick from window to window, down to the open sliding glass doors, as if expecting to see someone.

'There's no one there,' I say, 'and you know it. I've just come out of it, fuck's sake. I've already texted your missus from your phone, all twenty years of her. She's now not expecting to see you until tomorrow night. Sorry for wrecking your plans and all.'

And he watches me, points a finger, runs a hand over his face, tries to get a handle on this. He runs it over that large, firm round belly, thinking, digesting, pushing now that accusing finger through a vertical line of hair bisecting that greedy gut, taking a couple of steps backwards, eyes on me all the time.

'Okay,' he says, clearing his throat, ready to talk business. 'Serious now – what do you want?'

I go, 'If you ask me that again, I'll scream. In fact, I might scream anyway. It's not like anyone will hear me.'

And I'm walking the kidney shape and he's stopped there, central, watching me go round and round and round.

I say, 'I'm going to do this all day. I could do with the exercise. I normally hit the gym pretty hard three or four times a week, you know, but I've been letting it slip.'

'You a thief?' he goes, lifting a hand over his eyes, shading them from the half-hearted morning brights like a misplaced salute.

'No.'

'What are you then?'

'That's just a clever way of asking me what I want, isn't it? And I asked you not to ask me that again or I'd—'

And I fucking scream.

It bounces off the house, forces itself around his sprawling garden, dashes in among his shitty fake Chinese statues and wanky garden-centre leprechauns at the tree bases which, I happen to know, light up at night.

And now I chuckle.

And it's shocked him. He's dropped the hand from his eyes, has his arms by his sides. I have his full attention.

It's a curious thing when a person suddenly does not know what to do with their hands. It tells you that they're self-conscious, afraid. That confidence has been yanked from under their feet, right out of their muscles.

I'd say, right about now, Danny reckons he may have a maniac on his hands.

I go, 'Told you I'd scream.'

'Yeah,' he says, nice and quiet, 'you did. You see, I'm just trying to sort out what's happening here.'

'Very little. Honestly, very little.'

'What are you?'

I pause, take in some of the potential of this place, thirty or more acres of it, from beat-down, shitty pig farm to a barn with knobs on.

'Okay,' I say, 'and you're the first to hear this.'

'Yeah?'

'You ready?'

He nods, turning on the spot now, genuinely, passionately interested in anything I tell him. 'Yeah,' he goes, 'I'm ready.'

'I am . . . '

'Yeah?'

'An assassin.'

'A wha?' and it's the hand over the eyes again.

'An assassin. That's my job.'

'Who for?'

'I'm a government assassin.'

'A government assassin?'

'Yep.'

He says it again, 'A government assassin?'

Again I go, 'Yep.'

'Like James Bond?'

'Yep, like James Bond. Or Seamus Bond, if you like. Seamus Bond, licence to kill.'

I make a gun with my hand, fire a shot at the ground.

He goes, 'And you're here to kill me?'

'Yep.'

And he's turning.

'Me?'

'Yep.'

'Is this a joke?' he says, but I suspect he knows this is not a joke.

'No,' I say. 'Honestly. I swear on my life, Danny. This is not a joke.'

'So why don't you shoot me then?'

'Because I don't have a gun.'

'Wha?'

'I don't have a gun.'

'Why not?'

'Because I don't need one. Who needs guns? Guns mean crime, crime means police, investigations, blah, blah. That's not how I work.'

'How do you work?'

'In other ways.'

'Wha?'

'You heard.'

'Ah, wha? This is bullshit.'

'No it's not.'

'A government assassin? Seriously?'

'Yes.'

'With no gun?'

'Yes.'

'You're joking?'

I go, 'Danny, seriously. I am not joking, okay? Rid yourself of the idea that this is a joke. Please.'

And he has stopped turning now, instead turning just his head, tracking me as I come in and out of view.

'Jesus,' he goes, 'a government assassin,' as if to himself.

'Aye.'

'For what fucking government?'

'Irish.'

'Ah now, get away with yourself.'

'Don't believe me?'

'No.'

'Then watch.'

'Watch what?'

'Watch why and how you get killed. What other government would be arsed doing that with you?'

'How do I get killed?'

'It's very simple.'

'How?'

'Put it like this,' I say, and I'm walking and he's turning again and I'm walking and he's turning again, 'you are not getting out of that pool alive.'

'Wha? You think I'm going to drown?'

'I know it.'

'Fuck that.'

'Trust me,' I say. 'I'm an assassin. I might as well be standing here with a gun for all the difference it makes.'

'Yeah, right. I'm not drowning.'

'You are.'

'I'm not.'

'Yes you are.'

'How?'

'How do you think?'

'Wha?'

I say, 'It may be today, maybe tonight, maybe tomorrow, but

sooner or later, Danny, it's going to start to make sense for you to slide under that water and get it over with.'

'You fucking think so, do you?'

'I know so.'

'Never.'

'You will either do it on purpose or you will just be so tired and cold in your wee yellow trunks that you will just drop down and not find the will to stand up again.'

'Sure it's roasting in here.'

'It is now,' I say. 'But I've turned the heat off. It's going to get cold. It's November, Danny, and you haven't got a coat.'

'Fuck.'

'And when you're dead – and I will be checking you are really, doornail dead, dead as a herring dead – I'll crank the heat up again.'

'Fuck.'

'By the time someone finds you, Danny, you'll be like an over-boiled chicken and the ambulance workers will take selfies with you.'

'Jesus. Is this a joke?'

'Don't ask me that again.'

'Wha?'

'Don't ask me if this is a joke again.'

'Okay.'

'So are you starting to get the picture?'

'What picture?'

'Danny, you're a stupid cunt. I'm asking you if you're starting to understand what the hell is going on here?'

'Wha?'

'I've got all day,' I say. 'All day and all night and all tomorrow. Fact is, I've got as long as it takes.'

He's looking around the pool, seeing if it's possible to get to one side, heave himself out and make a break for it before I get to him.

'Can't be done,' I say. 'And you can trust me on that. I tested all this yesterday when you were wanking in your blacked-out Range Rover.'

'I wasn't.'

'You were. You went dogging.'

'I didn't.'

'You did. You watched some couple shagging in the back of a Ford Focus and pulled your wire.'

'I didn't.'

'Jesus, whatever. Does it really matter now?'

'Wha?'

'I really wouldn't worry about the dogging, Danny. Your life is coming to a close. Get, for once in your life, a sense of perspective.'

I fix the scarf tighter around my neck, shove my hands into my jacket pockets, and keep walking, keep being watched, keep providing the surefooted rhythm to Danny's exit.

He starts swimming now, thinking, swimming the few strokes back and forth and thinking. He starts telling himself this is a battle of wills and that he has the most to lose, that he will find the strength to go longer and harder at this than I can.

But there's a voice at the back of his mind, a voice that will get louder and louder, clearer and clearer, and it's telling him that he has already lost. And, as that stone-cold realisation begins to settle in Danny's mind, our little chat takes a long pause.

I consider how he will start to use my name soon, that he will start to humanise himself to me as much as he can. I consider that he will offer me a very large amount of money, that he will tell me to walk away with it and no more will ever be said.

But I have already thought of all of those factors, already

considered everything I can about this situation, a set of circumstances planned over a period of nine days.

The property's secure gates are locked, his mobile is on divert and the only person who will miss him believes he's on the golf course with his mates, who he's going on the piss with later.

I stop walking, and Danny stops swimming. We look at each other, and he figures I've already figured all of this. He is asking himself to be very, very clever, telling himself that's the only way he will get out of this.

But the voice, the little voice that is given life by a deadly sharp little device called instinct, won't let him not consider the fact that there is very bad news ahead.

It will already be asking him to prepare. It's telling him that sooner or later, just like the man said, he's going to need to start considering that the best option he has is to kill himself.

I take out a packet from my pocket, take a bottle of water from my little bag. I pop out a pill, put it in my mouth, swallow it down with a chug.

'Modafinil,' I say. 'Very useful. It's what you call a nootropic, Danny. A smart drug. Students take it for cramming. I'll be wide awake and focused all night.'

I put the packet and bottle away and start walking again.

★

Darkness is a few hours old and Danny is exercising from the neck down, just his head above the water, a man visible from his gold chain upwards.

He is shivering now, his teeth chattering, his face flicking little involuntary jerks as his muscles work hard to battle the deep, still, chill. The only mist now is no longer from the surface of the water, but from out of his mouth.

I've asked him if he has pissed yet but he won't answer. I genuinely wanted to tell him it might provide a moment's warmth, but he didn't speak up. He didn't like that I was pissing in his pool as I asked it, didn't chose to move into the warmer water I made.

I've asked him how hungry he is, and eaten a ham sandwich and Mars bar while I waited for an answer.

And I've asked him if it's true he beat a ninety-four-year-old woman to death, if it's true he likes the word to get around that he hires paedophiles and rapists as bailiffs?

He says now, 'You . . . can't bruise me. You can't . . . injure me.'

I don't know what the fuck he's on about.

I say, 'Wha?'

I'm sitting on a poolside seat, just watching and watching, and he says that to me.

I stand up, walk to the edge, ask again, 'Wha?'

He goes, 'It won't look . . . like an . . . accident if . . . you bruise me.'

And he starts moving to the ladder, his limbs juddering like some terrible disease has seized him. He's starting to think about climbing it, about what happens if he does get my boot in his face.

Speaking softly now, watching my own breath as the words come out, I say, 'Something really pretty about bruises, isn't there, Danny? Something elegant about the colour schemes, the way they change, the way they cover up the hurt in such a graceful way.'

He's wading, still trying to get to that ladder, all in slow motion, avoiding looking at me, and there's a splutter, some kind of cough, some kind of cry that speaks of more than just clearing his throat.

I say, 'Bruises are like a badge of healing, aren't they Danny?

Like something that says to the world, "I was hurt but now I'm getting better."

He reaches the ladder and I'm already there.

I say, 'Truth is Danny, you'd be doing me a favour. A bruise on the head would explain the drowning, wouldn't it? It'd look like you bashed your cranium, lost yourself for a moment, slipped underwater.'

He pulls back, waving his hands beneath the surface, trying to say something.

I say, 'In fact, come closer. Let me bash that head of yours. It'll hurry this shit up.'

He's twisting his head from side to side now, teeth clattering but nothing coming out.

'They say it's nice after a while, Danny,' I tell him. 'They say that after a while you begin to breathe the water in and out of your lungs like air, that it gets euphoric, that you feel high, that it's not the worst way to go.'

And instead of the shaking, his head is nodding, nodding, nodding.

I want to ask Imelda Feather if she would have the stomach to see this happen, if she would go the distance if she had to do this herself. And in part I think she would, in part I think she wouldn't.

But I can't ask anyone anything. My job is to do, not to question. I'm good at this stuff because I know the weight of that distinction, because I have the stomach for the separation of reason and role, because I have the guts, the on-off switches to do the shit that others want done but cannot do. That's the post, the accident game I have carved out for myself.

And here I am, upgraded, saluted, salaried.

I know why men come back from wars and never have a clear thought again. I know that minds are tainted by the kind of things I have seen, that neatly compartmentalising the explosive and unwieldy is not possible, that all that stuff has tamper switches, that being able to just shift it offside is a myth sold by shrinks and life coaches.

You have to do it yourself, to think your own thoughts day in and day out and find a way to think other things as you think them, to think some thoughts louder than you think others. You learn to live with what made you, with what was done to you and what you have done.

It's the *not* being it, the *not* thinking it that drives people insane.

It's the trying to stop the unstoppable that drains the life force out of heads and hearts.

★

We're touching 2 AM and exhausted Danny's eyes are closed as he slides, deliberately, carefully, under the water. It makes him look, for the first time, as if he has taken some control of this situation, and I almost feel proud for him.

I thought he might look at me, watch me watching him, try in some final way to make me remember this end of a life and feel in some way bad about it, his only way to try to impress himself onto my emotions. But, in fact, his eyes are all done with looking at the world.

Maybe my face is not the last thing he wants to see. Maybe it's too much to give, too much to allow me to know that he took my image to the darkest, deepest place a man can go.

Maybe he has a beautiful lover in his mind, an image of a place where he laughed, or of a loving mother, a proud father, a moment in his life he can see and is making him feel safe.

And, as he goes down, as the bubbles appear, as he starts

sucking in the water he paid for, I sing it. I sing a final, gentle, sweet tribute to a man heading off to his fate.

I go:

Oh Danny boy, the pipes, the pipes are calling,
From glen to glen, and down the mountainside,
The summer's gone and all the leaves are falling,
Tis you, tis you, must go and I must bide.

Chapter Two

Kerk Counselling Service
Amsterdam, The Netherlands
8 March 2016

IT'S EIGHT months before my night with Danny.

I've got age on my mind.

Age is the most amount of information in the least amount of space.

Tell me someone's nationality and I'll take a shot at what sports they like or what god they know about. Throw in their sex or race and I start refining the picture.

But the whole thing unlocks with age. Age is the mileage, the clock, the time, the fact, the base of what a person is.

Ask any doctor or cop, ask a journalist, ask anyone that needs to get or give hard information about people, about who they really are. They need an age. It says how long they've got, what they don't care about, if they're a threat.

A name is a retread of some random word someone else owned. A country is just a sound, just a lump of come-and-go habits. Age is the ID in your bones, the inside-out truth.

Fuck around with age, what happens? You end up paying someone to stick needles in your face and wearing stuff you can't wait to get out of. Then everyone starts lying about you looking younger and younger, when you look worse and worse.

Fuck around with age and sooner or later you become ridiculous, sooner or later you fall asleep or break a bone.

I'm good at age. I can guess yours fast, and I'll be close. I won't be scanning your clothes or refreshed follicles or half-arsed beard or ray-gunned teeth or shapeshifted eyes or asking how you feel, who your heroes are, what music you like. That's all void.

I'll be watching how you move, your limbs, fingers, feet, seeing how they all fit together. I'll be watching the way you are around people, around the bodies of the old and young, at the way you look at them and the way you don't.

Humans have been sussing out age since before we were humans. We've been needing to know the age of everything we see, eat, drink or jump off since we were apes. Age tells us what we need to know, and never more than when it's the age of another person.

You think you can trick the smartest creatures on the planet with ten minutes in a clinic? The only one getting fooled in that situation is the one paying the bill, the one in the chair.

So here's my point. If I say there's two males talking alone in a room, that means nothing. If I say it was two Irish guys talking in a room, it has no value. Two white guys by themselves and talking to each other, so what? There's no useful information there.

What if I tell you one of them was a priest? You're thinking, *Oh right, now we're getting somewhere – maybe it's a confession?*

What if I tell you one of them was fifty-two and the other was eleven? Now you've got a story. Now you know there's a different dynamic, now your mind is opening up to other possibilities, things based on the age of the people in the situation.

And, truth is, now you're thinking, *Is that eleven-year-old okay in there?*

You're thinking, *I shouldn't jump to any conclusions here, but . . .*

That's how Ireland has changed. That's where our minds go, because the whole country got punched in its sleep, the whole place woke up.

Back then, when I was eleven, I had no idea about age, about numbers, about how they tell a story. That fifty-two-year-old, he knew. He knew all about the numbers. The number was all he needed to know about someone to know if he liked them or not. Sex, creed, background, attitude – all irrelevant. If he had your age, he had the only fact that mattered.

I used to think that guy, Father Barry, must have been eighty or a hundred – as old as the hills. But I think of his gait and his skin now and I'm saying fifty-two, sticking with fifty-two. I can see him, very clearly, the way I saw him the last time I saw him. I see the crinkles, shades and sags, the lifts and drops of him going around the place and my brain goes, *Over fifty, not yet fifty-three – that guy's fifty-two.*

If I ever see a headstone with the words, 'Here lies a priest, died hard aged fifty-two,' on it, I'll know who it is. If I see one and it says, 'This one died hard aged fifty-five,' I'll not be so sure it's him. I'm *that* confident at this age-calculating stuff. I don't guess it, I say it.

I stood in his study one day and he told me age describes everything. He said that age says when you can start to design a dream and when not to bother. He said that age can be hope, promise and power and all sorts of other stuff, and I hadn't a baldy what he was on about.

He said to me, 'Age holds court over ugliness and beauty.'

He went, 'And, Aloysius, you should know that youth is beauty, they are equal.'

And I said, 'Okay.'

That was his thing, having me come into his study and stand in front of him. I'd stand for ages, legs getting numb, as he wrote in his book or looked out his window and hummed some holy tune or talked away to himself in Latin.

So, look, you wanted an example, a memory of an event in that shithole institution? I don't talk about that place – I've never talked about that place – but I'm going to say this much, and it's all I'll say about it. In all that lies ahead, there's no more talk from me about that place, okay?

Well, I had to stand in that study a lot, standing there looking at bookshelves, bibles and ornaments and golden Jesus figures and thank-you cards. It was like a fucking shop.

One day he said, 'How many breasts have you seen?' Honestly. That's the sort of shite he said to the boys there. Random stuff about parts of the body, often about breasts.

So on that day I had to think a bit because, being eleven, I hadn't seen many breasts. Then I told him I'd seen seven.

He sat back, put his big black shoes up on the chair at the side of his desk and said, 'Breasts come in twos, you stupid prick.'

I reckon he thought I wasn't being serious, that I was trying to make a joke, maybe trying to insult him. So I said 'Sorry' and then 'Six', and that seemed to make him feel better.

I'd seen the breasts of a woman on TV. I'd seen a nun's breasts. I'd seen the breasts of a drunk woman thrown off a train for stripping.

The single breast was when the sister of one of the boys came to take him away. Me and this girl, nineteen years old, sat on the waiting-room bench and chatted before he was brought to her. I saw the hatred in her movement as she talked about that place. She was wearing a black Motörhead T-shirt and as she left with her brother's wee hand in hers, she pulled it up, flashed a tit, beamed it right at me.

I always thought it was a lovely thing to do. It was like two fingers to that place, like some secret magic button, some sign to me saying, 'Hey Aloysius, one day you will find a whole wide world out there.'

But the priest would have went bonkers. This was a man who said women were to blame for all the sin in the world, who said nuns were wise only because they knew of their natural shame, who said females carried 'the devil's doorbell' in their knickers, that we were lucky to learn at an early age that women are 'rich with danger'.

So I switched my answer from seven to six. And the old goat dropped his head back, went silent and, I don't know, maybe let the image of six breasts gather some space in his sludged mind.

You have to wonder what it was for him, you know? Breasts ease, don't they? They ease and cushion and feed. They engage the senses, don't they? They make joy, they're incapable of causing pain. Was that what it was for him? Did he never know a breast in his life? I don't know.

Anyway, you wanted an example.

So he got up, walked to me, took my right hand, my little finger, folded it at its knuckles. He pressed the nail, pushing the finger back into itself, hard as he could. And it was sudden, colossal pain. Pure, sharp pain, something tearing up through the flesh in my arm. A sting that doesn't stop, a break that stays breaking.

I know now that's one of the pressure points, one little drop-a-man trick they teach police, teach bouncers. Everyone goes weak, anyone is all yours, when you bend and press their wee finger like that.

He goes, 'You dirty little bastard.'

He goes, 'You nasty wee bastard.'

And I shut my eyes so tight my face hurt. I opened them and saw this blur, saw him cupping and swinging his free hand. He clapped me over the ear so hard he knocked me clean over.

He always hit ears that way, Father Barry. He always caught air the in his palm, slammed it into your head that way, leaving you deaf and sore for an hour, leaving you with a headache like a brick had hit you. He always knew the best ways to hurt someone with nothing but his own body.

You get to thinking how, one day, you will turn the tables on a man like that. You get to thinking about reversing the roles, avenging it all. When you're eleven and he's making you stand naked in front of him all day and knocking you into bookshelves and trophies, you think, *One day I'm going to bash the brains right out of his head and all over the floor.*

But it's so hard to find a day when you can even look him in the eye. You struggle to find half the feeling you need to not run when he calls you. You're the opposite of him. You're the giant when he's not around, you're nothing when he's there.

You get to thinking that the only thing you can fight a man like that with is time, because you know one day you will be gone, out of there, away from him. And he knew I used to think about that.

He said to me one time, 'Months, weeks, days, hours, minutes, seconds, Aloysius. All of those little numbers are in my hands, all of those little facts – do you understand?'

It's tough when you have nothing to fight with, when you're

too small or weak or scared. Fighting back is as natural as rain, as natural as stones and trees.

But when you can't, the only thing you can do is take it to your dreams, to the only place where you can change things. You can lie down at night and float away to a place where you have what he has, where you can use fear and time against him, where you can reverse and avenge. And night after night I was killing that man.

You know, it's a funny thing, one of the funny things about what Irish children were put through by so many holy men and women. The funny thing is you never hear people asking, 'Why weren't some of these guys killed?'

You never hear that.

No one says, 'How did all of those fuckers avoid getting strung up, beaten to death or shot in the head?

'How come no abusive priest was nailed to a tree by the balls? How come no freaky nun was tied to a friggin' bonfire?'

People want to not look back, they work hard to reach a place where they beat off the volume of these people in their heads. Some people see it as a problem that was designed to be unsolvable at the time, designed to fit their weakness, their age, and they grow away from it.

But I'm generalising here, every case is different.

My case?

If you ask me how Father Barry survived?

He didn't.

That example I gave you?

That was the last time he hit me.

Chapter Three

9 March 2016
Birthday of St Aloysius

BEEP.

Awake.

Stars above. Hundreds of them, coming into focus, getting clear in the darkness. Neatly drawn locked-together luminous-penned triangles, over and over on the ceiling of the flat.

How and why? Who and why? How long did it take to do that? How sore would your arm get doing that?

I don't know.

A yawn.

Beep.

Another yawn, a short, angry one. I rub my eyes and say, 'Ninth of March.'

Beep.

I need to think about this flat, about how I am not getting used to it. A one-bed box, three floors in the air. I can't fully live in it, can't sleep long or deep in it.

Beep.

It always feels moments away from being cold, as if there's an open door or window I have never found.

The place came with total blackout blinds, with those secret Stars of David on the ceiling. It comes equipped with some story that is not mine to know.

It sucks the frigging life out of me, this flat. There's no welcome here, no sense that anyone has ever had a wholesome day in this place. It's not a space to think, and I'd like a space to think.

Beep.

They test vehicles in the garage below. It's the APK, the Dutch MoT, their NCT. Cars and car horns get checked every day from 7 AM to 7 PM, and I am losing my mind.

I remember I was never used to fancy-living. I stayed near an airport, getting a dirt-cheap house nobody wanted right under a full-on flight path and listening to magnificent jet engines climb in and out of my head, in and out of the sky, and marveling all day at the hands-down brilliance of aeroplanes.

Or even some abandoned coop by a good road, some crumbling brickwork kip at some half a highway where engines blend in and out of my personal space.

But no, this kip is my domain. It's like living in a checkout, in a dishwasher, in a microwave, in a reversing fucking truck where the sound is meant to annoy, to spit and stab.

Beep, beep.

Beep.

I'm thinking now about the faces I saw yesterday, the random bodies in Amsterdam, and I'm calculating people's ages by slashing numbers apart and throwing others together to find bits that fit.

And I'm lying here counting stars and beeps, adding up chunks of useless and chopping one sum from the other.

This mind, like a silent battleground, is the mind of a man who turned forty on this day, a mind that has three seconds worth of ambition today, one calorie of ambition today.

Beep.

I roll over and breathe in, nice and slow.

I reckon we're talking 7:10 AM.

And I close and open my eyes.

Beep.

I reach out for glasses, slide them on, lift up the faintly-lit luminous watch and can't be sure what I read because the lenses are so smudged, but it's about 7:10 AM. I throw off the specs, get out of bed, walk to the door, shrink my pupils.

Now I'm looking in the bathroom mirror at a man of forty-four, a man who was yesterday thirty-nine. I see a man who needs a haircut, a shave, a wash, a good night's sleep. A man who needs a style, a smile a—

Beep.

I shower and dress-flick on the TV, pre-parked on my news nipple of choice, where Germans talk about America and Europe like they're warring lovers.

Beep.

And that's the shortest beep, and there's a guy who always does short beeps. It's more of a wee blip, of a little toot, of a bee.

There's a double beep guy, a long beep guy, a mid-range-beep guy, a short-beep guy. And the double-beep guy kills me. His second beeps go like javelins into the ears. That double-beep guy's after-beeps have me turning up the TV, have me turning on taps and flushing the bog. That guy has me walking off into the shiny sharp-edged industrial end of Amsterdam to get my head out of this jar of a flat. I've looked at wooden floors in warehouses and chatted about the colour of garden furniture because of that double-beep guy. I've bought earplugs and sat, deafly, in front of the telly because of him.

I called my landlord one time, told him I can't be here anymore. I asked if he had another place which didn't have car horns funnelled into it for twelve hours a day.

Beep.

'It's like Chinese torture,' I said, and he went, 'No one ever had a problem with it before,' as if a problem has to have a history to be a problem, has to have a twin to exist.

'Who the Christ lived here before?' I asked him. 'Some deaf, nocturnal artist, some Jewish car-horn fanatic?'

He went, 'You know I'm too discreet to say.'

I'll have to move.

Beep.

I can't be forty and accepting this. I can't be forty and feeling like an intruder in my own home, can't be having alerts gunned into my ears when I'm trying to replan a life.

The only other person living in this building is the woman below, the mad-as-fuck old crone who shouts random shit out the window. She has a ghostly looking helper who comes to see her every couple of days, who takes her out like a dog for short walks around the local sights, to see the flooring warehouse and hear the beeps up close.

I look out the window sometimes, see them walking in or out of this place, and I don't know which one is which. I see them, both sixty-five, when I'm heading out sometimes and I don't know which one is mad, which one looks more crazy or caring than the other.

Beep.

But remember.

Remember.

The way my life is now, this flat works, blows cold on me, keeps me awake, insists that attachment is for some other time, some other place. This flat works because no one knows I'm here, because no one knows who I am. It works because it's all hard cash and no callers and you never see police, and because the attic door above my head leads fast to the rooftop. And the drop from roof to road is enough.

Beep, beep.

I'm closing my bedroom door now, but not all the way. I'm leaving a gap, the width of my palm. It's too narrow for any uninvited guest to pass through, too open to suggest they shouldn't bother.

The first thing I'll do when I get back is check it, put my palm on the floor and check if the door has moved, and that will be decide if I really should run.

On the street, bag over the shoulder, I head for the train to Schiphol Airport, thinking about beeps, thinking if I'll beep going through security.

Chapter Four

March 2016

IT FEELS like everyone has emerged late from the big, white north-European winter and shaken themselves down. It feels like they've all flown south to find some spring light, like everyone has done it at the same time and we've all got stuck in the big rush.

The big queue feels jammed, bottlenecked, and I have nowhere else to go. The only thing that can get me somewhere is the thing that's going nowhere.

It's been about forty minutes.

I look around now and I'm thinking flat-out about queues. I've been thinking about queues for forty minutes. I'm thinking just one person in front of you makes a queue. Six people in front, and that's a queue like my queue.

Five now.

Christ, come on.

And I'm looking at queue faces, poses. I'm looking at tired-legged queue people protesting about queueing without saying anything.

Another one from my queue goes forward, all polite and smiles, her passport open. The guy behind the glass has no interest. She's ready for him to look back up, and he doesn't give a shit.

Instead, the guy behind the glass looks up at me.

Second time he's done that.

Second time he's picked me out of two hundred people lined up in front of him.

I go as if I haven't noticed, as if my eyes aren't the best, as if they're resting in some middle distance and he just happens to be in the way.

I drop these eyes now, have them look at the back of the feet of the guy in front of me, get them looking at the maroon document in my hand.

Some Scottish girl behind is half-whispering about being fat, or about how she was fat.

She goes, 'It was like even my head was fat, you know? Like hats didn't fit?'

I look up and the guy behind the glass isn't looking at me now and I'm glad of it.

She goes, 'And it was like people actually hated me because of my weight, and that made me hate myself more, you know?'

I look down again, at the back of the guy's feet in front of me, at the passport.

That guy in front – some tired Dutch dad – has got cotton wool in his right ear. He takes a step forward, touches his ear now, as if he heard me think it.

Three left ahead, then it's my turn.

I fill the cotton wool guy's space and the queue loses a name, changes shape, changes length, holds the order, holds the thing that makes it a queue.

I'll take a stab at twenty.

Formerly fat-headed Scottish girl behind me is twenty.

Not easy with just a voice to go on.

Cotton-wool man is, what? Say, forty-four?

And I've caught myself again, weighing up patterns and calculating vintage. And I'm so fed up pushing this stuff, this useless adding and subtracting, around my mind.

She goes, 'I know Mia, right? You know the other Mia, right?'

The guy behind the glass looks up at me again.

Eye contact.

And I find myself suddenly dismantling my Mr-Average-in-the-Queue act and staring back.

Tick, tock.

And he stares too.

All right now . . . there's going to be some sort of incident.

Tick tock, tick tock.

And his eyes shift to the face of the woman in front of him. He says something, shoves her passport back like change from a drug dealer.

The girl behind me goes, 'I mean, how well would you say I know Mia, you know?

'I mean my Mia would text me a thousand times a day, you know what I mean? Text my head, right? I mean you do know what I mean, right?'

Cotton wool guy rubs his neck and I see unwiped boke on the right arm of his shirt, the fresh baby that did it is just ahead of him in his wife's arms.

'I mean, you understand me when I say "Mia" – you know who our friend Mia is, right?'

Fuck's sake, I can't listen to anymore of this.

I need to get out of this queue.

'I mean,' she whispers, 'B-U-L-E-Mia, right? Ana's friend, right?'

Her conversation is for a clinic, for a support group, for a quiet night in, not for pissed-off people in a passport queue.

Someone disconnects from the front and we all repeat, moving forward, one more foot of land secured, one foot deeper into the country, one minute older, one minute more fucking dead.

She goes, 'Haha!'

Cotton wool man sneezes, gets a side glare from his wife, the wee sleeping blob momentarily awake, briefly unfurling its face.

He's forty-five, I'm saying. She's thirty-six, I'm saying. I'd said forty-four but I'm saying forty-five. And I'd bet on it now. Man, I'm a black belt at pointless crap.

Glasgow girl goes, tiny whisper, 'This freak in front of me, right, seriously, is wearing odd shoes. I mean, not like nearly matching, I mean like not-at-all matching.'

This'll be me she's talking about, and I'm willing to bet she's not wrong.

Balls.

'I know, right?'

I dress like a man who would wear that cardigan at the bus stop, that hat you saw on the railings. I dress like a man who covers himself in glue and rolls through tents at festivals.

Lack of care, of class, of culture, lack of a good role model, an abundance of bad upbringing? Trying to blend in, trying not to stand out, trying too hard not to try?

Spin all those around, take your pick. Guilty as charged. I dress like a clothes horse, like a pizza. If you picked a homeless dog, a rebel mongrel, off the street and made him human, I dress like him.

She goes, 'I've never seen that in real life before.'

So what do I do? Get someone to tell me what to do when I get out of bed every day? Get an advisor, a guru? Follow a fashion icon?

Should I?

Go fuck yourself.

I hear a click, that fake camera noise on your phone, that retro shutter sound. My – no doubt – odd shoes are going live at this moment. They're bouncing off a satellite, ripping along some fibre-optic cable, bursting onto someone's screen.

Ta-dah!

I give it four seconds and look down, just to check. I may as well check.

Aye, that's me, yep. Last one to know, last one to the party. Odd-shoed. A sort of dark-yellow one and a dark-brown one. A partly formerly suede one and a non-suede one.

If I'm honest with myself, there may be other sartorial errors going on here. I have authored some great disasters in the past. This isn't the first time I've been tweeted, not my first Facebooking. Social media hasn't been good for me as a brand.

She goes, whispering, forgetting I have nothing else to listen to, 'I know – a sign of madness! There's a psycho axe-murderer here!'

That makes me smile a wee bit, and I'm smiling still when the man behind the glass looks up, right at my face.

And here you are, my passport-checking friend. May I present to you my smile. It started ironically, but now you're looking at it, it's become a big lie. But you can tell that, can't you? Your training tells you there's something dodgy about me, doesn't it?

He looks down and I feel so very ready to get the hell out of this queue, to take any route I can, to take the fast, short route, the mined route out of this airport.

The girl behind me goes, 'Send help!' And she's chuckling away.

I turn to the Scottish girl and her bulimia behind me – yes, twenty. And skinny and tasteless as a fork. She's twenty, and the last of her beauty has been sucked over and killed on the pretty bones in her face. She's twenty and she's done violence to herself. She's watched as violence drew her a rib cage, as it sharpened her knees and elbows, yet still she went back for more and more.

She shuts up, looks down at her shoes. I smile but she doesn't see it.

There's a whole big pause now, some silence I made her do, and I look back to the man behind the glass.

I have this dead-still face when I don't mean to. I have this face like a face that's been punched but got away with it, a face waiting for the next thing to happen. It's the resting face of a pirate on the ocean. It's bleak with wide, dark, soggy eyes and broad bones and broad corners, with half a dozen little life marks. You don't know if it will cry, this face. You don't know if it's menacing you, contradicting you, supporting you, if it's impressed or otherwise. This face is just stopped, just stationary, is not being anything.

Maybe the only thing you really see in my face is your face. It could be that you draw your own conclusions on my face. If you're happy, my face might look happy. If you're sad, it might look sad.

People look at my face sometimes like they're looking in the mirror, like it's cold and familiar. I see them looking around it sometimes, at its eyes and nose and mouth, and I'm always about to tell them their age, but never do.

And the guy behind the glass wags his finger and cotton-wool man with the baby sick on his arm goes forward and nods politely.

Whatever happens next, I will not nod at the guy behind the glass. I will show him this face, and this face on the passport, and he can take it from there, whatever way he's feeling.

Scotland girl is gravely silent. Maybe she died on the floor. She maybe just malnourished to death, heart-attacked to death, dropped dead gorgeous at the non-symmetrical feet of an axe murderer, a six-foot blank-faced blade wielder, a guy with persuasive shoulders and, right about now, the back of a shirt hanging over his arse.

The guy behind the glass pushes Cotton Wool's passport back, uninterested, wags my way.

I walk at him, right to his little office window, and stop that bit closer to the glass than I should. I close my passport over as I put it down, inviting him to show me if he has any thoughts on me, on who I am, what I am, because I would like to know. He looks at the cover, at my nation, then up at this face. He opens the passport, flicks to the page, looks at my 2-D face, back to my 3-D face, compares, contrasts.

I don't know if he's got something or not. I don't know if I'm on some list there, if I'm a flashing light, a red flag. He could know one or more things I don't want him to know, and I stand here waiting for judgement.

He's got this born-in-the-sun southern-European skin, this skin that looks like it will explode with hair. He's got eyebrows like thick moustaches.

And he goes, 'Happy birthday, Aloysius,' and looks up at me again.

He goes, 'It was my grandfather's name.'

He's thirty-four. Maybe just thirty-five.

I say, 'I'm sure he was a good man.'

He doesn't care now, slides the passport back, puts his eyes on someone else in the queue.

I step away, pass freely into Portugal, drop the shoulder bag on the floor, tuck the passport into a pocket, check my watch, stretch my back, yawn freely.

I roll my shoulders and pull the bag up again, begin heading for the bus to Faro.

Chapter Five

March 2016

ON A bus, changing into shorts, a T-shirt, matching trainers, sunglasses, a cap.

Out and walking a street where a guy can rent a bike.

I pedal thirteen miles, bag across my back now, rolling out of town, opening up muscles that have been jammed closed across this day.

It's a warm country road, east of the city, with lush greens and warm, dead patches of earth on both sides. It's a place for old cats and half-built houses and invisible noisy insects, for cold bottles of beer and big tomatoes.

Further along now and the scene ahead gets all strong: picture-postcard stuff, arty homepage stuff, vivid and clear. It's an image you just want to get into, a place you could go to suck up some high-quality air.

Rich green-and-brown woods to the left, a dusty grey road sweeping off to the right. Straight ahead, it's a field rising up from the horizon, a deep, bright few acres that, from this position right now, looks like a distant red mountain is sitting right on top of it.

I pull off to the left. There's a big iron gate in these woods, set way back. You can barely see it from the road, the rust blended in with the burnt-orange bark, the thick old iron bars like branches.

I get to the gate, pause under the patchy shade of the trees and bars, look around. I look far into the lean, beanpole trees on either side, up and down, around and about. Nothing. I look again, both sides, deep into where it gets dark, and there's nothing. To the best of my knowledge, no one in the world is watching.

I wheel the little vehicle into the trees, checking the time, and park it out of sight. I go to the tree I need to get to, the one with the helpful branches, and climb.

I snag my knee, a twig pushes me in the face, one jabs a lip, and I get to where I need to get. It's just high enough to see over the wall, just covered enough to be out of view if you look this way from the house.

The old soldier is arriving, right on time, 6 PM as always. I see the chestnut skin hanging from him, see how it looks like he is being vacuumed out of himself.

The old man in red Bermuda shorts is rolling out his blue mat now, stretching his arms. He's starting his pensioner yoga, all slow pulls and pushes for those who've done all their pushing and pulling. It makes him feel comfortable, helps ease the flow, makes him feel better inside.

He twists his grey head up to either side, looking over now right at where I am, staring solidly into the trees, and I am still as stone as he releases his neck and turns away.

The old man, his stomach hanging like a deflating balloon, walks to the blue pool now. He carefully puts one foot on the little aluminium ladder, takes a good grip, begins to climb. He pauses as his feet touch water, as the temperature meets him, and lowers himself more now. He slides quietly beneath, barely troubling the water, and he starts to hold his breath.

I check my watch again. Just gone 6 PM in Faro, just gone 6 PM in Ireland, and I was born right about now forty years ago. I'm forty years from the womb yet this Portuguese tree I'm sitting in has more plans and promise for the future than I do. I'm forty years breathing and I reckon humans have no business being this age, that thirty is a good enough number at which to drop dead in order to keep the human race ticking along. I'm forty and I reckon thirty is just enough to get the breeding and raising and fighting done, before the stupefying too-late wisdom sets in, before you get to the stage where you're an old man with a sack for skin, getting into a pool.

And I realise I haven't breathed in a while, that I've been holding my breath along with the old man in the pool.

So now I'm breathing in the beginning of a whole new year of this life, now life begins.

And I'm thinking how, under that water, that sunned old goat looks, more than anything else, like a huge shite.

Chapter Six

June 2016

I'M BEING smiled at by *Sunflowers*, their faces and lashes lifted joyfully in front of me. There's a bunch of people nearby but, for a few moments, I'm the only guy alive looking at this thing, these shaky, rough, vivid blooms.

And that's what I'm thinking about now, that's what I'll take away from this latest Van Gogh visit – the shallow consideration that I sat down on a bench and had this world-famous thing to myself for fifteen seconds.

Some guy sits beside me now and I say to myself, 'Grand,' get up to leave.

The fifty-odd guy goes, 'He got joy when he painted them. He painted joy into them.'

I say, 'Aye,' and go get a bowl of chunky soup.

★

I'm in the sunny city, taking in its pushed-together buildings, its high narrow streets, its deadpan browns and greys.

A woman on a bridge with a striking, well-organised Dutch face, is talking on a phone and wants the call to end. She looks into my peripheral vision, and I look at her. She waits a beat before she turns away, unimpressed. It's the unimpressed face we do to each other, a face that signals she is controlled and confident.

Or is it that, in this comfortable but Farmer-Joe shirt, in these off-trend trousers which no longer have an arse, I am some kind of brief spectacle for someone who is fed up with it all?

And all I've got now is two numbers, twenty-nine and thirty. I've got instinct asking me to choose, asking me to pick one as it hurls other stuff at me. Instinct says, 'She's single, lives close, likes to swim, can think in English, has a hundred million photographs on Instagram,' but I cannot know if somewhere deep down I'm just making it all up.

There's the clank of an old bell on a new tram, and I go get a malty Belgian beer in chunky glass at a Gravenstraat bar. I watch people – local, foreign, stoned, embarrassed, secret – and I count and count.

My phone rings, shivering in an inside pocket, and I'm thinking, *Who the hell is that?* I pull it out, see it's an Irish number, press ignore. I scroll through the website, the nihilistic Danish website I work for, to see what's happening with comments on my pictures.

They hire me, these mental Danes, every few months. They pay me to go and get images, to get stuff they say takes people apart and cuts and levels pockets of humanity.

Last year they sent me to Belfast to get pictures of drunk Loyalists pissing against walls, dressed in well-pressed band uniforms on 12 July.

They send me to European capitals to get shots of small-hour sex acts beside tourist sights, of women forcing drugs onto their unborns in train stations, of men's faces as they leave jails. They send me to hospitals and parties to get shots of people curled up in balls. They loved it when I came back with shots, for example, of a man trying to force a tablet into a bubbling wound he carved on his wrist.

The website – it's called 'People Are Clowns' – goes crackers for stuff that doesn't make sense, that's ironic or fucked-up. Its tease is to reduce, to boil the shit out of lifestyles, of human performances, until they're just bones. It says, 'Come and get it, come and see the bare truth, the bare arse of who we are.'

The screwball who owns it wants me to throw spears at matadors in Spain and come back with the pictures. He wants me to find druggies for a street party where everyone's dressed as Muhammed. He wants me to get lifelong teetotallers blocked and make them marry each other.

I like doing crazy shit for him, but it's getting to be a lot of work for very little cash, and I have a future that, sooner or later, I need to think about.

★

Walking home, I pass an Irish pub. Some guys, between twenty-nine and thirty-two, Derry GAA shirts, are finishing pints, ready to go find, lose, invent some memories, to look through red windows, argue over cash, make jokes about their closest companions.

I look past them, see a reflection of myself in the window – Aloysius among shamrocks, Aloysius walking alongside an arse-baring leprechaun, Aloysius, thirty-nine, with too much hair.

A guy, thirty, goes, 'Here, Worzel Gummidge. Want me to get ye a mirror?'

The whole crew of them laugh. I'm thinking not the city, thinking south County Derry.

I smile now, wave a hand and go, 'Enjoy your day boys.'

He goes, 'Aye, fuck off.'

I think how today I've seen both sunflowers and flashing neon shamrocks.

Whatever.

I put the phone to my head.

One message.

'Aloysius,' it goes, 'it's Martin Gird. You maybe remember me – I was one of the team in Dublin who helped you resettle in Ireland. Give me a ring when you can on this number. Something interesting to ask you. Right. All the best.'

★

In thirty minutes I'm sitting on my sofa and drinking a bottle of water.

The phone rings again, same number.

I can barely remember who this guy Martin Gird is and have no idea what he wants.

'Aloysius?'

'Yes.'

Sounds like he's in a pub.

He goes, 'Give me just one . . . sorry . . . sorry . . . so how's life with you? Long time no see.'

I read the long Dutch label on the back of this water, reading how the stuff in this bottle refreshed warriors of old on summer days. I'm reading how they splashed it through their dirty guts and declared war, how they got thirsty in the first place by romping with young maidens.

I go, 'Aye, long time indeed. What do you want, Martin?'

He goes, 'Listen carefully, okay?'

And I go, 'Okay.'

He goes, 'I want to introduce you to someone who can end this *pointless fucking existence* of yours. Do you understand me?'

I take another drink.

Chapter Seven

June 2016

NINETY MINUTES to kill before boarding, and I've never had a haircut in an airport before. I sit down, look away from myself as she crops, as she finishes off with a straight razor.

She goes, 'Where are you flying to?' and I say, 'Dublin.' She says, 'On business?' and I say, 'I don't know, to be honest. Just one of those go-with-the-flow things.'

On board and I have barely enough elbow room to spring open a can of Coke. I rub against the overweight man beside me.

I look to him, fast-breathing and sweating in his seat, and take a stab at forty-six, a stab at a five-digit BMI. I stab again that he has spent the weekend paying demanding Amazonons to adore or despise him, one of the two.

'Sorry about the squeeze,' he says, eyes closed, processing recent memories. 'I should've bought two seats.'

I take a Modafinil, wash it down with the Coke and watch as he grins to himself.

'You're grand,' I say.

I freshen up in Dublin Airport, brushing teeth and spraying under arms in the toilets. I see the mirror and select forty-one, run my head under a tap, paper-towel away the scratchy clippings from the back of my neck. The way the hair sits now, with these eyes whacked open, I'm a bit surprised to see I look almost like I should.

A taxi takes me to St Stephen's Green and I ring Martin, tell him I'm where I'm supposed to be. He picks me up nine minutes later in a fat Mercedes and I can't even guess what is going on here.

We turn corners quickly, a confident but stop-start route, as he pilots through busy, overworked, way-too-narrow streets.

He goes, 'Cars are like cholesterol, eh?'

I nod.

He says, 'Do you know Dublin?'

I go, 'A wee bit. What age are you Martin. About fifty-eight?'

'Jesus, great way to greet someone!'

'Aye, well, I'm out of practice being nice. Far off?'

'Fifty-six, so not too far off. Old before my time.'

Two years is pretty far off.

Martin's surrendered in the weight battle but is smart in a new suit and clean shoes, a gaunt yet round happy face, the look of the country in the city. He has eyes that once twinkled, now stained where they were white. He looks like a man who has smiled and winked his way through a few situations.

He helped me out a few years back, helped reconnect me with Ireland after years of travelling, helped me formally become a citizen before I left again.

I remember he was a good guy, a man who helped with complicated shit when he didn't have to bother.

There's no words for a while, and he goes, 'You working these days, Aloysius? Over there in Holland?'

I go, 'I'm living, as you told me, a *pointless fucking existence*.'

He goes, 'Yes, that's right. And that weird website you're working for! "People Are Clowns". Ha! Someone told me you were named as a snapper on that. I took a look before I called you. Jesus. People are clowns, that's for sure.'

He grins at me, says, 'Didn't hurt your feelings did I?'

I smile, 'You surprised me with your insight.'

He likes that.

He goes, 'You were in Belfast for all the marching and pissing then?'

'I was indeed.'

'All the drumming and shouting and the cops dressed like fucking starship troopers. Mad stuff, eh?'

And I say, 'Aye.'

I look into a wing mirror at the thick traffic behind.

'Are you going to tell me any more about this woman I'm going to meet?'

'No,' he says. 'I'll let her do that. And don't fucking ask her age whatever you do.'

He says that and I'm thinking mid-fifties.

★

We're on some broad, anonymous, well-tended D4 street when he pulls over, clipping a parking cone and urging me out. It's like there's a rush. He dashes around the car and I see no reason for it.

'I don't want to be late,' he says.

A converted Georgian house, three decks of offices, a front garden under cement. Number 39. The formidable black wooden door buzzes and clicks open.

'I like to be as early as possible,' he says as it closes behind us, its locks re-gripping.

'Fair enough.'

'Come on.'

We walk to the back, passing a main staircase, to where the floor creaks and the light fades. We pass instructions about fires and a room that smells of microwaved plastic.

A narrow flight of spiral stairs, some iron back entrance to the top floor, Martin first. No oncoming shiny patches on his arse, telling me the suit is reasonably new, or he's on his feet a lot.

Up top there's a bland, white landing, half as deep as the building. A huge window looking out over the backs of homes and offices.

One white wooden door – the only door – is to our left.

It hosts a black plaque: 'Shinay Associates, Ireland.'

Opposite the door, on the wall to our right as we step onto the landing, a painting – rich green-and-brown woods on the left, a dusty grey road sweeping off to the right. Straight ahead, a field rising up from the horizon, a deep, bright few acres, and what looks like a distant red mountain sitting on top.

I look once, now twice.

'Here,' he says, and pushes the door handle down. There's a beep, then a buzz. It releases.

A little reception room, a lean, bob-haired, secretary, thirty-three, just going for a pot of steaming coffee, smiling like a stewardess.

She nods at us, takes the pot and walks the short distance to the door at the back of her office, holds it open.

'Thanks Eunice,' says Martin, and we walk through.

The door closes, the sound of a firm, secure connection with the frame.

This room is big and bright, white walls and bookshelves and a globe, and two long, wide windows. The scent of cigarettes, of coffee, of people talking, the must of long hours. There's a fish tank in one corner, with no visible fish. In fact, there's no water in it.

A woman, fifty-nine, stands with hands together like a yoga instructor, looking hard at me. Her straight, lean face breaks into an easy smile. I smile back. She steps from behind her desk, walks to us. A blue skirt and blue blousy top: an outfit she's worn many times, an outfit on the turn.

Martin goes, 'Aloysius, Imelda. Imelda, Aloysius.'

She reaches out a hand and I reach for hers. Soft, bony. She has these nice blue eyes, this nice moisturised skin, some kind of silver-grey thing going on with her disorganised hair. She drinks, she works out, she works a lot. She's maybe sixty-five.

'I'll see you later then Aloysius,' says Martin.

'Thanks Martin,' we both say to him.

The door clicks open and he passes Eunice. She's bringing over two steaming cups on a tray. She smiles at no one in particular as she places it down, a little biscuit on the side of each white saucer. She lifts the coffees to the table, lifts the tray away and leaves.

Imelda raises both her hands, moves them around, inviting me to take a good look at the place. The solid clicking of the door seems to indicate the start of this, suggests Imelda clicking into place.

I smell soap now, some fresh air waving it around, maybe one of those home smells that you can buy in a can, one you spray when you're having a visitor.

There's a Gaelic pitch outside, behind where she sits, beyond the open window, and some urgent shouts from the field are carried now into the room.

'Martin tells me you're interesting,' I say.

'Good afternoon,' she says.

Maybe sixty-three, a maintained sixty-three.

'And what is it you do, Imelda?'

She has me sit down and takes her brown leather chair, her power seat to my lesser, wooden, padded piece. She takes a sugar cube, looks at it, drops it, stirs. She pushes a laptop out of the way, clearing the deck.

'Did you have a nice journey over?'

South-western accent in there somewhere, a touch of the Cork, but well marinaded in Dublin.

I say, 'Fine, thanks.'

'Get to Dublin much?'

'No.'

'It's a good city,' she says, 'has more than its fair share of fuckers though.'

I nod and say, 'Everywhere has that honour.'

'Thank you for being here,' she says, taking a sip, looking around my face, examining my hair, my neck, the bag I'm still holding, that I now put on the floor.

She says, 'You asked what I did?'

'Yes.'

'I assess people.'

'For?'

'Work. Different sorts of jobs. What is it you do, Aloysius?'

'I assess people too.'

She laughs at that, raises her eyebrows and nods as if to say something more, but doesn't voice it. I think she put lipstick on for this meeting, but she wasn't bothered about doing anything with the undone hairdo. Maybe she got caught in a wind.

Some guys on the pitch outside yell in unison, some victory or crisis on the grass, some act of violence or other.

She goes, 'And what do you assess people for?'

'Pictures, mostly,' I tell her. 'I've drifted into this sort of . . .'

'I know,' she says. 'Sort of providing sort of dangerous but levelling sort of photography for a sort of nihilistic website. It keeps you out of trouble, etcetera. Is that sort of it?'

I don't move.

She goes, 'It's called "People Are Clowns". And they pay you wages that a disabled Bangladeshi child could earn. Is that sort of right?'

I don't move again, and I don't like her.

She goes, 'I admire your commitment to your art, Aloysius, but I do wonder where your ambition lurks.'

It's not a question.

I notice that her arm hurts, maybe her shoulder, as she drinks again from her cup.

I reach for my cup, take a sip.

Some silence as our cups and saucers meet again, as I get my ducks in a row.

'You had your hair cut,' she says.

It's like she's drilling into me, into my head. Or at least trying to, to cut through the usual, to get me to say something unexpected, to start measuring me by my responses.

I wonder how and when she last saw me, saw a photograph of me, saw my hair. Maybe my passport shot, maybe via Martin.

I look at the biscuit and I'm not sure that I want it. I take another sip, maybe my final sip, and put the cup and saucer down.

I go, 'With respect, Imelda – it is Imelda, isn't it? Yes? With respect, tell me who the hell you are.'

Her nails have been manicured, but a few weeks ago. I can imagine her standing outside a pub where professionals go, smoking a cigarette, her ever-so-slightly husky voice telling stories of outmanoeuvring people. I can picture her raising a glass to getting the upper hand, to others following her lead and drinking when she says so. There is something faintly powerful about her, something even faintly mystical, something faintly gypsy.

'I'm a former journalist,' she says, 'a former tabloid hack. These days I run this agency, headhunting people for work, mostly government positions. I know what the market wants and I provide what I can.'

I look at the heaving bookshelf to my right, at the words I can see, at words like 'Almanac' and 'Political' and 'Europe' and 'Dummies'. There's a book by Darren Brown, one on Charlie Haughey, one on bankers.

She watches me, breathes in, says, 'I live close by, I have two grown-up children who live abroad, my husband is dead by his own hand and I work harder than any saint or sinner you can name.'

I see a book on Ian Paisley, a book by Delia Smith, a book about roads in Africa, something by Agatha Christie.

'Excuse me,' she says, and I look to her. 'Does that cover it?'

I go, 'No. I'm trying to find out why I'm here. And why you think you know things about me.'

She puts the cup down, the shoulder catching ever so slightly.

'Let's be honest, Aloysius,' she says. 'You wouldn't expect me to be interested in offering you some work if I didn't know what you did already, would you?'

I watch as a tiny jolt runs through her. I see it hurt as she sits back and closes her hands together, fingers up, in some power move some life coach taught her.

'Frozen shoulder,' I say, although it's a bit of a punt. 'You getting physio on that?'

She nods, 'I am, thank you. It was very sore at one stage but not now. I appreciate your concern.'

The hands go back to the desk, back to the cup. Then she changes, pushes it away. Pauses.

I'm going to give this five minutes. Maybe not even five minutes.

'Do you love your country, Aloysius?'

'Do I love my country?'

'Yes.'

'I don't know what you mean.'

'Your arse. You know exactly what I mean.'

'It's an odd question.'

'A straightforward one,' she says. 'Ask your gut, it'll tell you.'

'Do I love my country? Let's just say I'm not aware that I feel love for it. It isn't on my mind very much. I don't miss it when I'm away, and I'm always away.'

'Is that a no? I'm not sure you're being very straightforward. It is a simple question, as I said.'

'Do you love the rock that hits you?'

'Come again?'

'You heard. So how about you? Do you love your country?'

'Is your country ever on your mind, Aloysius?'

'Imelda. You?'

'Do I love my country? Yes, I do. I love Ireland. I love being Irish. I'm very often actively aware of being Irish and I always enjoy the feeling. Greatest place on earth, greatest people in the world.'

I go, 'Really?'

She goes, 'Yes. By a good distance too.'

And we pause.

She wants me to react. I'm thinking she just said something you would hear in a playground or on a toe-tapping St Paddy's night, but I don't say it.

'I don't,' she says, 'blame you for not thinking the same.'

I say, 'I wouldn't care if you did. You know, from what I recall, growing up where I did, love had nothing to do with loving your country. Patriotism was a corporate thing, managed by people who didn't much care for their countrymen, by men whose real love was, how do I put it . . . costume drama.'

'Ah,' she says, smiling, looking away, then back to me, 'the North. The separate room, the place where we keep the old paintings and books and flags.'

And I think that's an insult, but I can't be arsed pretending to be offended and she wouldn't be arsed apologising anyway.

She goes, 'I'm hoping you'll not talk about the whole house from the perspective of that one room, Aloysius. I'm thinking of a bigger Ireland, the land of saints and scholars. You know the one?'

I say, 'Yeah, I know the one. And I don't owe it anything. And that's what patriotism is, isn't it? Debt?'

And her eyes travel around the outside of my face again, onto my neck, to my eyes, and she's not saying anything.

'Are you interviewing me, Imelda?'

She goes, 'I think I probably know you well enough.'

And I know she cannot know me.

I go, 'Right, and I think I know you might just be a wee bit fucked in the head, if you don't mind me saying so. What sort of work are you thinking of offering me?'

Her eyes widen, but only to feign surprise.

She says, 'That's a great conversational style you have there, Aloysius.'

I shrug.

She goes, 'What kind of work? Well-paid, discreet, a job not everyone could do. I think it would suit your background very tidily.'

And I know she cannot know anything but the most basic detail about my background because no one on this earth could compile that information.

But I let her play.

'And the job is?'

Another pause. She looks away, to the bookshelf, scans some titles, making a point of having to think about this answer.

'Let's say – PR.'

'PR? No thanks.'

She smiles.

I go, 'Do I look like someone who is going to work in PR, in any capacity at all?'

She goes, 'Not a bit.'

'Well, isn't that . . . '

She goes, 'Don't take things so literally, Aloysius. You think I want you to work in an office, meeting clients and telling them how good some shop is?'

'You're losing me. You said . . . '

'You're dressed, Aloysius, like someone who might arrive to service a horse and cart, like someone who might start talking to himself at any minute. You've got hair clippings around your collar, despite your half-baked efforts to clean yourself up. You look like you styled your hair in a public toilet and through a fucking hat. You look very much like a man who doesn't care about himself, and a man who doesn't care about himself doesn't care about anything. If you came up to me and said you were in PR I'd tell you go and stick your head up your arse. Now is that a good answer to the question you are struggling to find to ask me?'

I go, 'Yes.'

She nods.

I go, 'Funny enough, Imelda, if you came to me and said you worked in PR I'd think you meant palm reading. You could just about pass for someone who, when sober enough, sells made-up bullshit that passes for opportunities. See, I've flown in from Holland for this silly wee meeting, so unless you stop pissing around right away I'm going to mark this up as a mistake. And your hair looks like it's upside-down. No offence. How's all that for a response?'

She puts her head on one side, as if she's about to try hard to connect with me, and smiles, goes, 'None taken, yet I do think you're a complete prick with the social skills of a trapped fart and I want you to leave right away.'

And I'm not sure I was expecting that.

I stand up, grab the bag, turn away, reach the door.

She goes, 'Do you know your Yeats, Aloysius?'

I turn. She's looking at me, stern but pretty, planning to recite some old balls, planning to get all meaningfully Celtic as I exit.

I say, 'Wise up.'

I pull the door, pass Eunice and grab the handle of the far door. A tiny buzz releases it. Eunice didn't look up from her computer, didn't see anything she thought strange or unexpected. Eunice doesn't offer a goodbye.

The door soft closes and hard clicks behind me and I shake my head, ready for the stairs, for the Dublin evening, for the rest of this crumbling day.

And that painting – rich green-and-brown woods to the left, a dusty grey road sweeping off to the right, a field rising up from the horizon, a distant red mountain – is right in front of me now.

I go cold because I have climbed in those trees to watch over the wall where the old man swims. I freeze and know it is not even possible that this is a coincidence. It is not even possible that of all the images in the world, they have this one, here, in front of me right now.

I have to move on, I have to shake this shock away and go down these stairs. I must be mistaken. I'm seeing things. Places look like other places all over the world.

I get to the front door, hit the buzzer and Yeats hits me, the words I should have said thirty seconds ago.

I should have said, 'I will arise and go now' just to annoy her as I left the office.

Chapter Eight

June 2016

IN A shopping centre looking at shite on T-shirts, considering my options, and my phone goes.

Martin Gird says, 'I'll see you at your hotel bar in ten minutes.'

He's grinning when I walk in five minutes later. He's in the corner, tie loosened. His hand goes up, then curves round and points, like an ostrich's head, to the barmaid.

'Will you take a pint?'

I go, 'Fizzy water.'

Martin calls to her, 'And whatever he said, thanks.'

The Slavic barmaid, topping off a pint of Guinness, nods as I sit. He shakes his head at me as a cap is tugged from a bottle, rolls onto the floor.

'Well that didn't go too fucking well,' he says, that Dub accent thicker than I'd noticed before.

We say nothing as the barmaid drops off the drinks. She's twenty-four.

He lifts his glass. 'Here's to the day. *Sláinte.*'

'*Sláinte*, Martin.'

I drink and he doesn't, sets his pint back down.

He looks at my water, it dawning on him that it's not beer. He leaves it. Then looks back to it.

'You never settled back into Ireland,' he says, not asking it.

'Twenty-odd years away, give or take, as you know.'

He goes, 'I do.'

He goes, 'Imelda Feather.'

I go, 'That her name?'

'It is,' he says. 'She's accident prone. If she's driving her car or climbing some steps, it can all go tits up any moment, y'know?'

'Right.'

'I've learned that about her,' he says, turning his glass around, looking at the perfect line forming between that painted cream and black.

'She could be standing somewhere and something will fall on her head, y'know? She could bump into a Wi-Fi signal, that woman. She's attractive to bad luck, to accidents and incidents, y'know?'

'Right.'

'Do you know what I mean?'

'I do.'

'I mean, fuck's sake, she walked into a press conference I was looking after one day, Department of Health, years ago. She was paying no attention at all, writing something down, fell clean over someone's bag, fell onto some fella from the *Daily Star* and stabbed him in the chest with her pen. The fella had to go to hospital. He was near killed by a biro.'

I say, 'Jesus.'

'And you're wrong about the frozen shoulder. It's not that. She drove out in front of a motorbike a couple of weeks ago and he slammed into her.'

'Okay.'

'Aye. So that's what happened her shoulder.'

I nod.

'The lad's all right,' he says. 'The insurance will cover it, but he's needing a lot of physio. Fuck knows what'll happen, could end up in court.'

I go, 'Martin . . . '

He goes, 'She'll probably quote Yeats at you and fuck it up. It happens a lot. She doesn't know the words too well but quotes away all the same.'

'Right.'

He looks up, closes his eyes and goes, 'I have met them at close of day, Coming with vivid faces, From counter . . . '

'Martin,' I say, 'fuck up.'

He chuckles.

'I'm having you on,' he says, chuckles some more. 'I'm just letting you think I'm a bollocks, that you know everything about me before I start giving you a few straight facts, y'know. I'm softening you up before I hit you with the hard stuff, y'know?'

And he takes a deep drink, his eyes closed as a quarter of a pint is pulled into his mouth.

'Jesus that's terrible,' he says, exhaling and reaching into his inside pocket, taking out an iPhone.

'Now here's what I have to show you here,' he says. 'Just wait a little second,' he says, plugging in a code.

I look around. The bar is big, square, bland and blue, scented with bleach, scrubbed clean of atmosphere, of colour. With thirty minutes notice it could be a shop, a classroom, an operating theatre. There's no one here but us and the barmaid, who is flicking the TV stations around, searching in vain for something better than rubbish.

He goes, 'Look at this, eh?'

I look at his phone – a head-and-shoulders picture of a blonde woman, twenty, maybe twenty-one.

A smile, 'Bit of a looker, what?'

'Who's she?'

'You don't know?'

I shake my head, take a sip of clean water for my dirty guts. 'Should I?'

He swipes, another image. The same woman, laughing now, wearing a baseball cap. Swipes again. Family picture, a picture everyone has. A few more family images. One with a cat, one eating popcorn, one standing in the rain, one with Ajax playing in red behind her.

Then an unexpected one – with her legs open, lying back, laughing, a limp arm across her forehead, her bare vagina on display in the low light.

'We're getting to the bedroom scenes now,' says Martin, chuckling.

He swipes more. A blow job. A beer bottle. A Bavarian-style barmaid's outfit. Then what looks like jizz on her face. Then breasts on show in Paris, then some kissing with another girl in a nightclub. There's handcuffs, straps, a strap-on. Then she's asleep with her underwear down, on display without knowing it, taking digits.

'What's this about, Martin?'

'Revenge porn,' he says, still swiping. She's sucking two dicks, She's got '*schlampe*' written in lipstick across her back. She's being held by the throat, one with blood under her nose, one where she's being held by the hair, clearly in distress.

I put my hand over the screen.

'Thanks for the drink and the flight and the hotel and the porn, but I don't want either you or Imelda in the rest of my day. You got that?'

'Understood,' he says. 'Before you go, Aloysius, tell me honestly – you've no idea who she is, do you? Not a clue?'

He puts the phone down.

I sip, 'As I said . . . '

'Right. Well that's something. That's something amazing, to be honest. You see, that girl is called Maya and she had this boyfriend, this rich lad called Kris, who was a bit of a dick, to be honest.'

'Martin . . . '

'Listen to me, Aloysius. Just one more minute, okay?'

I sigh. I sip.

'So it didn't end well between Maya and this fella Kris after he started hitting her, y'know? After he started doping her and forcing her and freaking her out. So, he didn't like getting dumped, this fella, and he made a little plan to make a fool out of her, to stick some intimate personal pictures all over the Internet, you know? All this stuff I've got here on the phone, y'know? Some of them embarrassing, some a little more troubling than that.

'So, Kris was pretty methodical, went to about twenty porn sites of all flavours, uploaded the lot, included Maya's name, her home town, a link to her Facebook, asked anyone who was having a wank to this poor woman to share the dirty pictures, y'know?

'Took no time at all and she was all over the place, and no time after that until everyone knew. Everyone in her home town and all. All very uncomfortable, as you would expect.'

I nod. Sip. 'Yep. And . . . ?'

'So Maya's very upset about the whole thing, Aloysius. She tries emailing and ringing the websites but it's a hopeless task dealing with fuckers like that. Technically, she doesn't even own the pictures to ask for them to be taken off the Internet, y'know, because she didn't take them herself, you see. Ends up, she goes to her parents, Rick and Elena, a decent pair of people from Utrech, in the Netherlands. You've maybe been there.'

I shrug.

'So Rick and Elena aren't the least bit happy with this situation either, again, as you can imagine,' he says. 'There's not a lot they can do right away, but they start the long haul and get a lawyer and some IT lads on to it, and see if they can begin to sweep the pictures off the Web, y'know? In the meantime, Rick, her dad, takes a little notion, maybe a wee bit fuelled by anger, to look into this fella Kris, to get a good handle on him. He gets some of those IT lads to trace what they can, to see what he's been up to, and it comes clear soon enough that Kris is no stranger to doing this sort of thing to his exes, to knocking them about and getting pictures. In fact, Kris has been at this revenge porn thing for a few years, drugging one-night stands and hookers, scaring the shit out of them, taking their pictures. Our Kris here has got himself a bit of status among these knob pilots, a bit of a reputation in the revenge-porn community, for want of better terminology.

'Anyway, Maya's dad Rick finds this all very upsetting, and can be told of no bigger cunt on earth than this fella, Kris. And Maya's dad finds himself taking a wee look around online to see if he can get someone to, y'know, sort this Kris fella out. A decent father would be protective of his daughter like that, you see.

'Now Rick is a bit of a headstrong businessman, knows his own mind sort of man, and is happy when he finds this ad deep down and tucked away there on the old deep, dark net, y'know, deep in the hard-to-track corners of the Web, y'know? He finds this ad and he has a wee anonymous email exchange with a bloke, you know? And he has a chat with this bloke. It was an ad for what they call 'Military Services', Aloysius. You know what I mean? It was an ad that said the person could 'hard solve' your problems. It's not the sort of thing you would be looking for if you wanted to put someone in a bad mood, or wind them up or ruin their day, y'know? It's more heavy duty than that, a bit more of a fuller job than that.'

Martin sits back, takes another deep pull on his pint, sits forward.

'So anyway,' he says, smacking his lips unhappily, looking to his iPhone, 'here's a nice picture of Kris before he starting fucking around with Maya's life.'

Kris, shaggy-haired, trendy, good-looking, a white funnel neck sweater, a goatee beard, is on a Dutch street, is laughing.

Martin points at the image, just so I'm totally sure who he's talking about.

'It's Kris, okay?'

And I nod.

'And,' he says, 'this is what happened to Kris.'

The side of a neck, a thin rope pulled tight, a deep furrow into his skin cutting off blood and oxygen to the head.

Says Martin, matter-of-factly, swiping, 'And then this.'

Kris's face, tensed, as the rope bites harder, shutting down his life.

'This.'

More shots of the neck, shrunken yet more by the rope, the face flushed with the effort of fighting the unstoppable.

The strain, the bulging, staring eyes.

Then fingers trying to dig their way under it, scrambling to pull it away.

I don't want to see this.

'Horrible,' I say.

'Yes, awful,' says Martin. 'What a way to go, eh?'

He swipes again, this time to a video, and lets the film roll.

And I can hear it now, the gasp as the rope tightens, the raspy effort to suck in or blow out air, the oily, wet cry for help spilling from the closing tubes of Kris's throat.

The wider picture now, the hoisted Kris trying to loosen the noose, his feet, toes pointed, trying to find the floor just inches below him. His jeans are down, his underwear, as he kicks, fights for his life, eyes wide and filled entirely with terror.

The camera walks around him now as he struggles, a compilation of revenge porn footage and images rolling in a loop on an open laptop on the nearby desk.

And the kicking tapering off now, the dying sighs of a man fading away as his life ends.

'Now that's revenge porn,' says Martin, chuckling. 'That's pure fucking revenge if I ever saw it.'

He shakes his head, stops the video, takes a drink.

He goes, 'Atrocious stout,' wipes his mouth and looks me dead in the face.

'And it was you, Aloysius,' he says. 'You hauled that lad up there with a rope, you played that film to him. It was you who recorded this, who made this wee snuff movie. It was you who killed him, Aloysius. It was you who waited for him to stop kicking, who lowered him back down, left him slumped on the ground and shoved a plastic cock up his hole just so the story was crystal clear. You killed him as hard and as bad as any man could kill another man for doing wrong. It was you.'

I screw my face up. My eyes narrow. Lips curl. I'm almost smiling at what he just said. A kind of a shocked almost smile.

And just so I'm hearing this right, I go, 'Sorry, say that again?'

He sits back, looks around, happy with his work. He puts the phone back into his pocket, takes a drink, knows I'm watching him intensely.

He fixes me again, says, 'The police found him a week later. They found a scene that asked no questions of them. They found a wanker who wanked himself to death, an auto-erotic asphyxiation hand shandy thingamajig, dildo and all, an open-and-shut case.'

I nod and say, 'You've lost me, Martin. Seriously, you've lost me.'

'But I haven't though, have I?' he says. 'You did that to Kris, and there's no doubt about it. And the interesting thing I'm starting to establish here today is that you did this to him without even knowing who he was, without even knowing what he did wrong. How in the name of fuck, Aloysius, could a man be so hard to someone they don't know? What kind of a man has a passion like that in him against a man he knows nothing about? You knew nothing about the revenge porn, did you? You knew nothing at all about Maya, about the young man you did that to, did you? I can see it in your face, Aloysius.

'Sure that could have been the nicest lad in the world you were strangling there, couldn't it? But you didn't give a fuck. You ended his life and made his legacy nothing but a dirty, open secret. Is a few euro enough to make that all okay for you?'

He looks over at the barmaid, ducks in closer to me now.

'So tell me the truth,' he says. 'Tell me. I want to know. What in the world is it that you have inside you, Aloysius? What is it? Eh? What's the hidden, dark, dark bit of your heart all about, eh?'

I go, 'Martin, this is ridiculous and offensive and . . . '

He says, 'Where were you for all those years after you left Ireland? What was it you learned? What did they put in your head over there in Chechnya? What is it that you have been doing? How do you learn to do that sort of thing over and over again, and still live with yourself?'

I go, 'Okay Martin, stop there. Time out. That's enough. You tell me what this is about or I'm walking away. Tell me because . . . You ask me to Dublin, you ask me to meet some nosy woman, you show me porn, someone's murder, you . . . '

He goes, 'You never asked me to pay your flight, Aloysius, did you? When I asked you to Dublin on the phone you never said, "Ah Martin, yes, you're a great man, pay the plane and get me a nice hotel up by the park and I'll be over to meet Imelda." You just said to me, "No problem, Martin, I'll come to your meeting in Dublin." '

I go, 'But you did pay for the flight and hotel.'

He goes, 'I offered to. But you were coming anyway. You were coming anyway because you have money, you have a few grand about you, don't you?'

I shake my head. 'I'm skint.'

'No,' he goes. 'You act skint. You have a good few grand tucked away from doing a good few jobs like this neck trick.'

He lifts his pint as if to toast me, takes a drink.

'Still fecking waters and all that,' he says, winks, drinks.

'Go fuck yourself,' I say, and I have what will be my last drink with this man.

'I'm not a policeman, Aloysius,' he says, putting his glass down, smacking his lips again. 'I'm nothing like that. I did thirty-five years in the fucking civil service and I hated it. I worked for minister after minister and every one of them was a fucking asshole, you know? Every one of them. And the fucking red tape – Jesus – it would eat you up, eat your soul and chew it up and spit it back at you, you know?'

He rubs his head.

'I don't do any red tape now at all,' he says. 'I never write anything, sign anything – nothing like that. And I've never been happier. I just have this bit of a thing now where I help out Imelda with her business, just the odd job here and there, going to lunches and making the odd call. I love it. And I do what I can for her, you know? She's a good woman, a great woman, and you could trust her with your life, so you could. Honest to Jesus, she's as sound and solid a person as you could find, you know?

'And I'm solid enough myself, Aloysius. I hope you can see that in me, that you can get that from me. I'm not a snoop or a spy or a liar or anything like that. I'm just a man doing a job he enjoys, and he enjoys it because it doesn't chew on his soul, you know?'

A pause.

He goes, 'Will you meet her again? Will you give it another go? If it doesn't work out, we'll say no more. I'll never contact you again. I promise. If it does, well, I don't think you'll regret it. That's the honest truth – you won't regret it.'

I push my bottle towards him.

'You have told me today, Martin, that you think I'm a murderer,' I say.

'I have,' he says.

'That you reckon I got money to do . . . that . . . to a man I knew nothing about.'

'I have said that, yes.'

'And of that you are, you're saying, certain.'

'Yes,' he says, taking a drink, adding, '100-percent certain.'

I go, 'You're insane. Goodbye Martin. Goodbye, good luck.'

And I go, 'And keep that promise. Never contact me again.'

He shrugs, says, 'Fair enough.'

Chapter Nine

Amsterdam
The Netherlands
August 2016

PHONE ALARM.

5:30 AM.

I'm dressed, eating scrambled eggs, downing coffee, at 5:47 AM. I throw on a coat, set basic security traps, reach to the top of the flat's front door as I'm going out. I've cut a deep, slim pocket into the wood and, with two fingers, I tug my work mobile out of its hiding place.

I lock up, go quietly down the stairs, outside, plug my head into a black woolly hat and suck deep on the cold, dark, street air. I walk fast, head down, shoulders up, to Vondelpark.

The sun starts soaking up the night as I get to the tree, as I stop and look up to Tall Marianne's tenth-floor flat.

There's a red vase on the windowsill inside which says she has no reason to think there is a problem. I cross the road, look at the camera, get buzzed in, take the lift and knock the door.

Tall Marianne answers, eyes half closed, topless, jogging bottoms below, thirty years, three thousand late nights. She has a skinhead, a healed knife wound on her fake right boob.

The floor inside says she has been doing a jigsaw puzzle and drugs and reading about confidence. It says she has been drinking wine and tequila and rolling among all of that while holding someone close.

I close the door and she opens her mouth, the SIM card pushed at me on her tongue. I take it, she goes back to her warm bed and she'll be asleep in ten seconds.

I'm fixing the card into the old phone and walking among the debris of her just-ended night, towards the window I looked up to. On the sill I see the red vase, a US passport, a wallet, some coins, some paper dumped and crunched from travel. Whoever the American might be, he or she has had, I don't doubt, a brain-boiler of a sexual experience.

I click the SIM card into place, look outside, down to my tree.

Two men standing there.

They're looking at where I am.

I freeze, take stock, commit them to memory, step back slowly.

I say, 'Fuck,' and my heart makes itself known.

Jeans, jackets, clean, white, sober, alert, late thirties.

'Fuck.'

They have no business being there at this time, looking like that, looking in the direction they are looking.

I leave in silence, shun the lift and take the stairs, going up.

It could be coincidence.

On the next floor I look out again and they're still there. They're looking somewhere else, checking the sightlines.

On the next floor, they're gone.

I reach the thirteenth landing and lean against a wall, stop moving. I listen.

Listen.

Listen hard.

There's nothing. No clunk of the lift, no shoes on stairs, no words bouncing up this concrete block from the ground, no swing or shut of a door anywhere in this little tower.

I look out again, can't see them anywhere.

I count to twenty and again listen, listen, listen.

I see nothing, hear nothing.

I start walking down the stairs, becoming pugnacious, getting ready for hard and fast, ready for confrontation, filling with shove and luck, and my heart slips into its stride.

At ground, I watch the glass external door, take stock of everyone and everything I can. Nothing here tells me anything is wrong.

Four minutes later and a daybreak tram is coming, the whirr of it closing is the only sound. I exit the building. Two cars pass. I walk fifty feet, to where the tram is stopping. No one gets off. I get on, flash my card.

Nine people, none of them interested in me, none of them at the back. I sit in the last seat and try to see the whole city around me, try to see men in jeans who may or may not be trying to destroy my life.

Six stops and I exit, walking alongside Keizersgracht, self-briefed that my human engine is on some kind of starting block, some adrenal launch pad.

Three Englishmen and four Englishwomen, early thirties, are walking and laughing, trailing luggage, heading home. I stroll a few paces behind them, switch my body language, match their happy gait.

I slip on my glasses, pull out the phone, finally checking it. It tells me I have no emails, just one message from three days ago. I look around, 360 degrees, put it to my ear and, nice and clear, a woman says, 'I would like to order the potatoes, the vegetables and the beef in Munich, please.'

I press delete and pull away from the walkers, veer off to the left, towards the nearest canal side.

My gut, the brain in my gut, has me raise the phone as if busy, so that it won't look so wrong if I stop and turn, if I need to act crazy, to shout or run. I check behind again.

They're there, the two men, 220 feet distance, watching me, matching my gait, not too close, not too far from their target. This is no coincidence; this is a crisis.

I walk backwards for a moment, pretend I'm talking, move a hand in demonstration, watch them watching me.

I act more now, put an arm out, chat away, laugh loudly, rub my head, stop, lean against a wall. I spread out, chill out, become a guy who takes up too much space, the most relaxed person in the place, the alpha male, the too-confident guy you would look away from because you know he will not let you look for long.

But they don't look away.

I lock eyes with one, some flat-nosed dildo with a donkey jacket, and I'm slipping the SIM card out, sliding it into the fold of my right palm, now taking a firm grip of the phone.

The bigger guy, the bald one, is staring too. Whatever Flat Nose and Big Baldy are doing, they are going to do it very soon.

'Fuck flight,' I say to the phone, 'fight.'

And I welcome in the feeling bigger than fear, the feeling that covers and smothers fear. I feel the limitless entering my limbs and urging me forward now. I push off the wall, hard walk right at them.

I go, 'Looking for me?'

The bald one holds his hands up, goes, 'If you want to be found, we'll find you.'

English. Midlands.

He's the bigger one.

And he's the target.

The smaller guy with the flat nose laughs, 'Or we can *not* find you, whatever you want, mate. Up to you.'

English. South coast.

And my way of walking is making them uneasy. And the rhythm I am giving this situation is making them get ready for risk, making them brace for the throb of the fray.

Big Baldy puts a hand on his chest, poised to go get something in that coat if he needs to. But only if he needs to.

I put my arms up.

'No,' I go, 'it's fine, you can find me, lads. Here I am. Right here in front of you. Front and centre.'

And they're thinking fast, maybe getting confused, as I close in.

I go, 'Here I am you fucking cunts, moving into your point blank.'

They part, splitting the target, nervous smiles, but they're competent – they've done this before.

I'm imminent now, still fast.

Both are going to go for me, but I've got pace and, as a matter of fact, I'm strong as fuck.

They're looking at the legs.

I slam the end corner of the phone onto Baldy's crown, turn and elbow back hard as Flat Nose is grabbing, ramming his face.

I slam Baldy again, again, again, and my arm is being pulled back, my leg being kicked.

I slam again, hard as I can, stabbing him with the blunt edge of a phone, and he's dropping to the ground, his blood jumping now, little red dolphins into the air. He's thirty-eight.

A hard whack on the head stuns me. I turn, get palmed in the chin. My tooth cracks, break. I step back, keep balance, regroup. Bastards.

Flat Nose has pulled out a firearm, a pistol, but he does not want to use it. He jams it into my flesh, right to where it's too hard into my guts to shove it away.

One fierce, unexpected lightning knee in the balls, one serious, cupped-hand slap on his ear as he dips and he's deaf, dazed, aching. And I know he is under orders not to kill because I am still alive.

I whip off my glasses, fold the arms, jab them hard in an eye. Jab again, twisting. I slap the same ear again, this time throwing him off balance. The glasses are lodged into the head now. He's thirty-six. I let go and punch those specs, finish that eye off forever, stab his brain. He falls back. Another boot in the balls.

I check – both down, both out.

I want to put one of the fuckers in the canal.

I'm going to put one of the fuckers in the canal.

But I can't. They would die. That's a bigger story. Keep the story below the radar, out of the water, off the agenda.

I pull the bloody glasses out of the hole in his head and now I'm moving fast and breaking the SIM card in my hand, the taste of blood inside my face.

Now I'm a hard-running target in the centre of the city. Now everyone is coming awake and looking at me, now I'm in deep shit. Now I've got to start the escape plan.

Who are they?

Rounding a corner, looking backwards, bashing into someone – male, twenties – a bicycle, knocking him off, him roaring in fury as I keep going.

I cross a road, look back and there's no one. I run on, cross two streets more, a hard right, looking back.

No one.

On Rokin, towards the bridge I need, pulling in first behind a row of shops, behind a restaurant. There's an alley.

Stopping. Between big restaurant bins. My back hitting a wall, looking left and right, left and right, hands shaking.

I spit, a blob of blood. I wipe at the sweat. Off comes my jacket, white T-shirt below. Off with the cords, leaving just the joggers' shorts. I pull the headphones out of the jacket pocket. I open a bin, dump the jacket and cords, the hat, run my hand around the neck of the bin, close it, run my greasy hand through my hair, slicking it back then spiking it up.

I jog out the end of the alley, head down, earphones, trying to tune out the white noise of adrenaline slamming around my system.

And my pace is relaxed.

Look at me – the professional, working out before working.

And there are tears in my eyes, tears coming as I know I'm on the run, as I gear up once again to get the hell away from whatever it is that could burn and bury me alive.

I cough, a film of bloody phlegm around the inside of my mouth, my throat choked with iron and oxygen flavours. And I feel dirt coming up from somewhere, bits of grit and filth crawling onto my tongue.

I jog and spit, looking at no one. I jog in among emerging people starting their days, and I'm smiling, smiling as I turn around, running backwards, seeing no one, tilting my head side to side to the music.

I get to the bridge, cross it, turn right, two barges along. I turn and don't see them, don't see anyone who is looking at me.

And I drop onto the barge, go up to the front end, drop to the floor, my back against the red and black of the prow. I reach behind, flip open a little plastic hatch, take out a key, unlock the door on the floor, slide it open, fold my legs up, roll over and drop down, crunching as I land in the tiny salt-storage compartment.

I get onto my back, facing upwards, lie still, stay silent in that black cube. I look hard at the blue-and-white square of new-day sky above. I reach to my right, wipe and wipe at the sticky, damp-sucking salt and pull up a plastic bag. I pull out the gun, raise it to that sky.

It's here, now, that I stop. That I wait. That I swallow blood and wait.

I rub my face.

And wait.

I sweat and wait.

And I say, 'Stop, stop, stop . . . ' when more tears come into my eyes. I wipe at them and say, 'Stop, stop it.'

And my stinking hand, my restaurant waste hand, my rats' piss hand, wipes again at my tears.

And nothing happens.

And nothing happens.

Sweet nothing happens.

I blink and get my eyes as clear as they can be and nothing happens.

And then I see something moving, arriving right above me, some kind of bouncing light, something sky-coloured high in the sky, something flying, stopping, silent, secret.

And my normal mobile rings.

6:45 AM.

It rings.

And I lie here. Folded and secret, stunned at everything.

It rings out.

I wipe some sweat, more tears, knowing that this newborn day might close tighter yet.

I think about holding my ground, about dominating the environment, about flicking off the safety catch and fighting back, about being first to strike. I think about the pulse of war, about the thump of action I can bring crashing into any situation.

And it all turns to nothing, all melts away in my head, all runs down my face.

I breathe deep, keeping that pistol aimed at the sky, tilted right at that alien thing right above.

And the phone rings again.

And I know it will ring and ring and ring.

I get it with my left hand, number unknown.

I go for it, cough and collect myself.

I go, 'Hello?'

She goes, 'Hello Aloysius. It's Imelda Feather.'

I have nothing to say.

This disastrous event has to involve her, but I have nothing to say.

I want to say, 'Oh hi Imelda, I so much enjoyed meeting you, you're such a lovely person.'

I want to say, 'Hi Imelda, it's not a good time because I've got a drone following me and my life is over.'

I want to say, 'Fuck off and die, Imelda.'

Maybe I could ask her to talk about sitting in an office doing some nice PR, about going for a nice lunch together in some cramped Dublin restaurant.

And no words pass between us.

And someone's on the barge. Some footsteps, slow, careful, on the deck, heading towards the hole I'm in.

Step. Step. Step.

She says, 'Aloysius. That is a replica gun you are holding. You bought it in a shop in Bruges for €38.99'

More footsteps.

She goes, 'The man you are about to see above you is holding a real gun, but he can't be completely certain that your gun isn't real.'

And he's walking.

'If he feels threatened by you, Aloysius, he will kill you.'

His shadow arrives, climbs up me, up over my chest, my face, his toes right to the edge of the hole. I see the hands, steady and holding the gun, moving into place, pointing silently, ferociously, down at me.

I blink as he becomes clear, as I see how the blood has run all down his bald head, all down his face, around his neck, onto his shirt collar. And I hold my fake gun at him, and I hold the phone at my ear, and I hold my breath.

And the weapon feels so light now, so stupid, a child's toy in a shaking, adult hand. Another tear exits, slides down my face, drops onto the crisp salt bed below.

She goes, 'Lower the weapon, Aloysius. Would you ever, please, lower the bloody weapon.'

He goes, 'Five, four, three . . . '

I say, 'You win,' opening my hand, the weapon falling, sticking into the crystals around me.

He continues, ' . . . two, one.'

She goes, 'Brace yourself.'

And a boot crashes onto my wet face.

Chapter Ten

August 2016

SHE'S TWISTED around, firmly looking at me bunched in the corner of the back seat, hard-pressed against a door that will not open from the inside.

Martin is right beside me, also glaring, in the big, thick Mitsubishi four-by-four. The guy in the driving seat, the bloody bald guy who slammed his size twelve onto my face, flicks his eyes at me in the mirror, pulls them away. And does it again.

The blood has crowned him, spilled downwards, bits of dried trickles, spikes and lines left after a half-arsed clean-up job. His head has been split at the top, bone cracked, a coin sized slot. He should get that looked at.

'Are you sad, Aloysius?' she says.

I look at her.

She goes, 'You've been crying, you know. You were out cold and crying. Very strange. People cry when they're sad, don't they?'

Martin goes, 'Or happy. It could be that he's just a very happy man.'

Silence.

Imelda Feather says, 'That's such a good point, Martin. So, are you happy or sad?'

I am trapped, tense, jammed in this big machine. We're parked further along from the barge, from my blown hideout, my now-ended start point for a full and complete escape to another new life. Cash, ID, clothes, it's all in there.

Martin says, 'Who owns the barge? We'll be finding out, but you can tell us now if you like. It's not yours, is it?'

Imelda goes, 'I bet you it belongs to your Dutch friend, the transsexual bon vivant. What's her name – Tall Marianne? Would that be right, Aloysius?'

I'm not contributing. Not yet.

Martin goes, 'Does Tall Marianne still have a cock, Aloysius? Or do you know that much about her?'

Imelda looks at him, says, 'What's your interest there, Martin?'

She looks at me, goes, 'He's asked three times now if Tall Marianne has a cock. I think we've found Martin's happy place.'

Martin laughs, 'Sure I'm always happy. Crying with happiness half the time, just like yourself, Aloysius.'

Baldy with the busted head looks at me once more. I'm thinking how he'd shoot me in the face if he wasn't a paid player for these two.

I look at him, say, 'Where's your mate?'

We stare.

'Getting patched up in hospital,' says Imelda. 'He has lost an eye, by the way. There could be some deeper damage too, but it's too early to know. I believe you misplaced a pair of glasses, Aloysius.'

Martin goes, 'Which is a tiny bit ironic, when you think about it. Losing an eye to glasses.'

And Baldy still stares at me.

Martin goes, 'I've said it before – you can be a very angry man, Aloysius. You've a short fuse there, fella.'

Imelda says, 'And another fact about you is that at this moment you're stinking, you know that? Fucking rank, to be honest. You smell like a festering toilet.'

Martin agrees, 'You do. It's bad now, to be honest. You've got some kind of grease on your face and your hair and your sweat stinks like rotten onions. I'd say that fecking 1970s jogging outfit you have on you there hasn't seen a washing machine in a decade or two. When did you last have a good wash?'

Imelda goes, 'Stinking. Humming. Fucking hanging. You're a challenge of a man, Aloyisus.'

Martin says, 'If we take you to a nice hotel, let you get a nice shower, give you some nice fresh fashionable clothes, give you some painkillers for that broken tooth, buy you an excellent lunch, will you give us the afternoon?'

Imelda now, 'No more running and catching and punching and toy guns and all the rest of it. No restraining. Just chatting, just some grown-up stuff. A nice, pleasant, businesslike afternoon in Amsterdam? How does that sound?'

I nod towards the guy in the front.

'If he gets in my way again,' I say, 'I'll pull his brains out with my hands.'

'Wayne will go away if he's not needed,' says Imelda. 'Is he needed?'

And he's burning up in front, he's white hot with the urge to smash me to pieces, and he's having to turn his eyes away from mine in the mirror.

Suck it up, fucker.

Imelda's waiting for my answer and I go, 'Wayne will not be needed.'

★

He takes us to the Grand Krasnapolsky Hotel, Dam Square, drives off, pissed off. Martin takes me to a suite while Imelda goes to order coffee in the downstairs cafe.

I take his eye. He's leaner than when I last saw him, likely been on some diet to save himself. 'You said last month you wouldn't contact me again, Martin,' I say.

He goes, 'I didn't contact you again. Imelda did. I just happened to be in the car when you were dumped in it.'

It's a five-star hotel this, a five-star space, some cosy, clean, casual designer clothes, cotton-rich stuff, laid over a bed.

He says, 'Shower, shite and shave, all the stuff you need is in the bathroom. We'll see you downstairs in a half hour. If you run, Aloysius, then you run. Just remember, we're not the police. We don't have any bad news for you, okay?'

He holds up the key card and I take it from his hand. He holds up a box of paracetamol and I take it too.

'Let's have a bit of trust, eh?' he says.

'Who are you, Martin?'

He goes, 'I think you know we're serious, Aloysius. That's all you need to know. Just give us your full attention, okay?'

And I think that's probably something I will do, but I don't say it.

★

I'm neat, smooth, clean and, I think, on-trend and age appropriate in expensive, easy-going jeans, tan casual shoes, a blue-and-white striped shirt, a dark-grey sweater. I'm feeling and smelling good as I drop down through hotel floors.

Their chase is over for today and they've won, and it's very clear that I'm the prize. Yet I don't know why, or what for.

Doors slide open and smiling tourists towing luggage give me the space to walk out.

'*Danku*,' I go.

I can see the back of Martin's head in the lounge, a window seat onto thriving Dam Square. Every inch of it is under the feet of visitors, of groups in matching tops, of half the nationalities of the world mingling and watching puppets and pigeons and mimes.

There's a pot of coffee, some exquisite little biscuits waiting for me. The chair is wide, more comfortable than I'm used to.

I sit and pour coffee as they watch me closely, saying nothing, barely smiling.

I suddenly catch a fresh whiff of my own smell, whatever it was that had been left in the bathroom, and it's a calm and easy but wide-awake scent.

'For some reason,' I say to no one in particular, 'you two are seriously into me. Isn't that right? For some reason, you are very keen to go really far out of your way, with your wee double act, to get my attention. I reckon you need me to do something for you, something not anyone could do, something only . . . '

And I sit back, hold court, take a drink of coffee.

' . . . a person with no obvious connections, something only a disposable person could do. How's that for an opening statement?'

Imelda goes, 'You think of yourself as disposable? I don't. Try valuable.'

Martin nods, 'Valuable, yes. Or indispensable is maybe even a better word for it.'

And I take a drink.

'Tell me about this PR job,' I say.

She's in flat shoes, hair all standard windswept and undone and all over the show, a long blue coat she has thrown over a free chair, without a care as to how it ends up.

'Who is this gentleman?' she asks, a hard little stare at me, confusing me, even annoying me a little, those blue eyes taking too much of my attention. 'Where did that scruff go?' she says. And she smiles now, a smile that says she is pleased with what she sees.

She turns away, looks to her coffee, turns back, a suddenly different, suddenly more official look.

'PR job?' she goes. 'Sure I haven't offered it to you yet.'

I shrug and eat a very small biscuit.

She says, 'But yes, it is in one way all about PR. It's about reputation, just like everything is about reputation.'

I say, 'Whose reputation?'

'Ireland's.'

And I'm thinking how she can't know much about me after all, not really. I'm thinking she's misinformed, that she's still misreading this entire situation.

Martin says, 'Do you love your country, Aloysius?'

And I go, 'Pleading the Fifth.'

He goes, 'Because of what happened when you were a kid?'

And I say nothing.

We all take a moment, look out at a clanging tram, at a stoned couple laughing uncontrollably as they feed a bird who is wise to the drill.

Imelda puts her cool hand on mine, says, 'Let's go for a walk.'

Outside, her wrinkled coat under one arm, her laptop bag over a shoulder, Martin watches from the window as we disappear into the crowd.

She asks, 'What's spuds, veg and beef in Munich?'

'A good dinner.'

'It was the message on your phone, the one you picked up this morning, wasn't it?'

How in the hell?

She goes, 'It was the order from your latest client, wasn't it? I reckon you're an à la carte assassin, and this client has just ordered the full works. He asked you to come up with a cruel ending to your victim's story, just like you did with that Dutch lad that Martin spoke with you about. Am I close?'

I go, 'You and I both know fine rightly that I have no idea what you are talking about.'

I shake my head at her. No way lady. No way, lady of sixty-four, you know too much already.

She takes my arm, steers me towards a little cart under an archway. She fumbles in her coat pocket for coins, asks if I have any. I don't.

She finds some and the guy gives her a little, sweet pie. She inspects it, takes a bite, inspects it again.

And we're walking now, strolling, the city sounding like a busy playground, the big grand Centraal Station ahead of us.

'I hate to bang on but isn't that the craic, Aloysius?' she says, 'That someone has this morning confirmed a hit in Munich. That's what that spuds, veg-and-beef message means?'

I shake my head, about to speak.

She goes, 'I'll let you in on one of my secrets.'

Dipping into a whisper she goes, 'I know who the target is.'

And I know she cannot know.

She goes, 'He's a dog fighter. The worst in England. And he's going to be in Germany next month. My guess is that the client is some good-hearted animal rights sort, someone with a few grand

to spare, someone who has dipped into the coffers and found someone to do some very permanent damage to this horrible person. Or,
as you put it in your advert, they have a problem you can hard solve.
Isn't that the term you use?'

And I let her keep going, let her just fling open the gates and
rush it all in before I start the stocktake.

'Anyway,' she says, 'this conflicted, compassionate person did
a search, got in touch with you. And soon, I'd bet, you're off to
Oktoberfest in Munich, probably under the pretence of taking
pictures of drunk people for that shite website you work for. And
then you're going to find this person and kill him in a way that
will bring joy to those who hate him. You're going to do spuds
and veg and beef to him. He'll probably end up looking, more or
less, as if he has fallen into a combine harvester. And it'll have
been an accident, of course. You will make it look like it's just possible it was an accident, not something or someone the police are
going to put too much work into. I think that's about right, is it?'

A group of Irish pass, fresh from the train station, springing
on their feet, happy to hit the comfy crazy streets of Amsterdam.

She says, 'So now you know some of what I know.'

And I'm people-watching, adding up ages, letting her roll on.

She goes, 'But in order for me to explain more of what I know,
I need you to give me something. Because when you give me
something, I will give you something, do you understand?'

An elbow into my arm.

'Do you?' she goes.

More quiet.

'I need you to say yes,' she says. 'I need an admission, a private,
private, private admission, and then I can give you something.'

And I say nothing.

She goes, 'Say yes, Aloysius. Just say yes. One word and you will start to unlock this whole thing. Say yes.'

And she stops, this pensioner girlfriend on my arm, this somehow scandalous woman. And she tugs me to stop, and she is staring up at me, staring at my mouth from six inches below, and I feel like smiling.

And I know in my heart there is so much weight around all of this, so much hanging over me. I know how it is all so heavy that I sometimes wonder if I can carry it, yet I know that if it all ever crashes down I will not survive it.

I think how I have a solemn promise to myself, one among many, that I will not tell a living soul about this thing.

She's tugging my arm now, pulling me away from my own comfort zone, and she goes, 'Aloysius, just say yes and I will tell you I'm on your side and we can move along.'

And I would love someone on my side. But my side is so fucked up that I don't know if anyone else could handle being on my side.

She goes, 'You know I am not police. You know my interest is more complicated than black or white. You know I am serious and well-informed. It's time to engage with me.'

I go to open my mouth, still not fully sure of what it is going to say, and nothing happens. I don't know what the next thing is, I don't know now where I'm going. My gut is divided, my instinct torn in two.

How does she know what she knows?

Imelda tilts her head that way she does, looks as if she is straining to hear me, and her blue eyes – almost navy, always shiny – are like weapons, truth machines designed to make me talk.

'I'm maybe a little hard of hearing,' she says, 'but I saw the lips move on that inscrutable face.'

And she's good. She's good because I am starting to like this moment, this terrible leap-in-the-dark minute that seems like she is offering light, that seems like she is offering everything she has in her soul.

Somehow, from somewhere, my mouth opens and breathes in and says, quietly, 'Yes.'

She nods matter-of-factly.

She goes, 'Yes you do these things, yes you are planning this thing? Yes you are for hire to hard solve, yes? Spuds, veg and beef is what I said it was, yes?'

And I go, 'Yes', and nod at her. 'Yes, Imelda. I am these things. Yes, it is what you said it was.'

Now she watches me, looks all around my newly clean front, at the happy, scented hair falling around on my head, at the man she has somehow caught and washed and dressed and broken today, that she has upgraded and reworked so very quickly on this salient date.

I don't move, don't speak and I think of what I have just done.

And I wait, part of me braced for the hand on the shoulder, the thud to the back of the head, the stab of regret to cut through me.

But we just stand there, in the tiny wind, the accuser beginning to beam at the confessed killer.

'Good,' she says.

She tugs and we move on, turning left, down narrowing, packed, colourful, clean, dirty streets. She talks in underdone sentences about the layout of the city, about how, when she was a newspaper editor, she used to come here with her staff, get them stoned, get them laid, and they loved her for it.

She says she was so proud to travel with a bunch of happy, partying Irish people, the collective fizz of the Celts fired her up with joy, yet how she was always so happy to get back home to Ireland, even from a city she loved so much.

'I cannot be without Ireland,' she tells me, and I know she means it from deep inside. 'We are so good,' she says, 'so fucking good that when we produce one complete bastard, it brings us all down.'

One time, she says, she came with her husband, that he had been so embarrassed when he asked about hiring a prostitute for a threesome. And she laughs to herself, leaves the idea hanging, and I won't ask.

'Let's get stoned,' she says, and it's an interesting idea.

We smoke a fierce joint in a soft coffee shop with big beanbags for chairs, with pop art images of Bob Dylan and Sean Connery on the walls. It takes two minutes before I'm not sure if I will be able to stand up again, and it doesn't feel right to say to the ageing woman opposite me that she may find herself sunk into that beanbag for the rest of her days.

'Beanbags are the right thing and the wrong thing for a coffee shop,' I say, and she takes a deep draw.

'Well said,' she says, holding it in.

I go, 'So is *this* an interview?'

She goes, 'Yes.' And laughs, running a hand through stray, mad, silver-grey hair.

And I feel my head falling back and I laugh too, laughing too loud as some bass-based music begins surrounding us, pounding softly, kindly in our ears.

Some others, some younger people, look at us and we are making them laugh and wonder.

She puts her nice eyes on me, nice and wide, and we have a warm, easy contact.

I'm weirdly happy with how this crazy day has gone, how it is going.

She says, 'Did you google me?'

I go, 'I googled the shit out of you. Didn't really answer anything though.'

She rolls the joint around in her hand and smiles.

'I've had,' she says, 'both a terrible time and a wonderful time in my career, in my life.'

I ask, 'What was terrible?'

She goes, 'All in good time, Aloysius. And I'm sure you'd say the same to me.'

I say, 'You said you already know everything about me. Maybe what you picked up from a hacked call or two, from one of your rented drones, but no more than that.'

She nods, looks away.

There's thirty seconds of silence, of packed, stoned emptiness.

I go, 'You know, if you're setting out to set me up, for whatever reason, I'd have to say you're doing a very good job.'

She looks at me, smiles, 'Could you please stop suggesting I am being underhanded. That's not what I'm about.'

I say, 'Seriously? There has never been a hand more under than what is going on here, fuck's sake.'

'Fair enough,' she says, taking another draw. 'I'd say it feels like that from your side.'

She rubs her face now, checks her phone. It seems inappropriate that she breaks off, starts checking it for emails, for texts, for missed calls.

I watch her and it annoys me.

I take out my phone, do the same, pretend I have something going on in my life other than this high, beanbag meeting.

She looks up and a big smile works across her face, causing my face do the same. We nod at each other in silence, two people who have made a connection, who have started something.

But still there are no answers.

She goes, 'Take my calls, okay?'

I'm about to nod and she says, cartoonish Wild West accent, 'I gots to go.'

I watch as this woman takes one last draw. She blows the smoke out, pulls her arms in and, captivating the whole shop, rolls onto one side and pushes herself gracefully up in some almost-gallant move, some powerful yoga move. She stands tall, exhales some more, brushes herself down, pulls on her coat, and I feel like clapping.

She nods again, nods to others in the shop who are watching her, spellbound by her, and she collects her bag, walks out.

This woman has, on this day, killed my head.

And I let some words roll around my killed head as the door closes, as I see her confidently, albeit completely stoned, head off back to whatever it is.

My killed head spills back and my eyes slide closed and I feel baffled, euphoric, safe.

And I wonder now why she doesn't just say it, why she is so direct and indirect at the same time. I figure I have at least one thing on her, one thing I know now that she cannot know I know.

My head all heavy, all hanging upside down, I say in a full whisper, 'She wants me to kill Irish people.'

Chapter Eleven

Amsterdam
October 2016

ONE MONTH and nothing, no communication of any kind from Martin or Imelda.

I've spent too long wondering what the hell all that was about, wondering why I said yes to her, why I confessed. It allowed her to walk away knowing too much, yet I still know too little.

To be honest, it's left me feeling flat, low. It's the sadness of an unimportant loss, it's the small disappointment of being followed then unfollowed, it's the secret disappointment found in a ceasefire, in the end of a siege.

I've done very little since, nothing at all really. I've looked at Van Goghs and tourists, I've had a handful of Belgian beers in Dutch bars, I've sat in my part of Amsterdam counting the seconds between the beeps, I've got my tooth fixed and I've often looked up and wondered if there are silent machines watching me from the sky.

Yesterday I held the door open for the lunatic who lives downstairs, the old fool who has taken now to punching herself when she opens the window and shouts at the city. She was with her carer, and finally I got to see which one is which. The carer said to her client in Dutch, 'Say hello to your neighbour', and the woman looked at me, spat in my face, called me a '*kut*', which sounds more or less the same in English.

I wasn't even mildly surprised. The carer, who has the same face as the crackpot, wasn't either.

'She is in a bad way today,' she told me. 'She finds it hard to sleep at night and has done too much hitting herself in the face.'

I said, 'I know the feeling,' and scooped saliva out of my eye.

'Diane has Tourette's,' she said, 'a very disabling and complicated case of it, makes her appear very intolerant.'

'It's just a label,' I said, 'we've all got a few labels stuck to us. She just is who she is.'

'Yes,' she said, 'she is. Labels are how we make sense of life, I think. I'm diabetic, brittle-boned and a haemophiliac.'

I nodded, reckoning these two ages are going to be hell to really pin down.

There was some silence, maybe a little grumbling from Diane, maybe some swilling around in the mouth so she could gather up some more gob for me. I was sure she was about to let rip again.

'Don't worry about it,' I said, still holding the door, 'I'm much worse.'

'Are you ill too?' she said happily.

'I think so,' I said, 'but not in a debilitating way, in a stronger way, negative strong. I feel good and avoid diagnosis. I let the world just suffer me instead.'

The carer smiled. 'Medication comes in many forms,' she said. 'Press on, Mr Irishman.'

'You too,' I said, 'both of you. Press on.'

And she had said to me exactly what I was thinking, exactly the sentiment that had been going through my head as I came down those stairs.

Press on.

I re-engage with the most recent client, firm up the details, buy some heroin from a friend of Tall Marianne's in the Red Light District and go to Munich.

I cycle into the north of the city, pulling in at a lay-by used by people with full bladders, empty stomachs, tired eyes or roadside sexual fantasies.

I park up the bike, sit at a picnic table, drink water.

A German woman, forty-five, head down in a black overcoat and cream beanie hat, gets out of a mud-caked yellow Mini and walks towards me. She puts on some kind of fake tone, fails to make eye contact, asks if I like to eat spuds, vegetables and beef. I take off my sunglasses and I tell her I do. I say the textures all complement one another and she nods, acknowledging our understanding.

Her eyes flick to an insignificant looking tree on her left, to some stones gathered around its base.

She says, 'Hofbräuhaus, then this address at Eurobizpark. Tonight.'

She gives me a folded squared of paper, hunches her shoulders, turns.

I say, 'Dead on. Remember the stars.'

She nods, not looking back, hands shoved into pockets, never wanting to see me again, walks to her car. I see someone else in there, someone else in the car, their shoulders hunched up. The engine starts, they indicate, drive off.

I drink more water and wait, watching the cars go by.

Five minutes later and another car in the lay-by pulls away, leaving me alone. I go to the tree, as if to take a slash, and pull a plastic bag from under the stones. I tuck it into my shorts, get back on the bike.

In minutes I'm back in the city, among the busty, frothy signs for Oktoberfest, soon moving in among the early starters, the early singers, into the early strains of the *ooom-pa-pa* of the smart, mighty beer-bucket binge that is Oktoberfest.

I get rid of the bike, change my clothes in a pub toilet and check the bag the client left. Six thousand euro, used notes, tightly coiled in an elastic band. It's my rate; it's high, but it's a premium service. It's a service where police can't even be sure they're looking for a killer or not, one where suspects don't need to feel their lives falling apart as they think up excuses. The law needs a murder before a motive. My work cuts the truth in half, into quarters, slides it all away to places where it's too expensive, too pointless to look.

My targets are the personal, the people behind the private grief, pain or plain old monumental annoyance. They don't make headlines, don't create pressures, just make for catchy stories on websites. Their deaths are certain but the cause is blurry, freaky, even funny. Their deaths are little more than comment pieces, pub chats. Their deaths don't easily get linked to anyone, and if they do then that person has an unbreakable alibi because they really were not there.

I insist on one tiny meeting and one phone call, which must include three clear words, two months after we email. It builds trust, ensures that the person has the commitment to press ahead, gives time and reason for hot tempers to die down.

I want 100-percent payment in cash up front, close to the time of the job, the safest deal for everyone. That way, when the job is done, people – whoever they are, whatever their names – feel as if they've got more than they expected to get, feel like they weren't taken for a ride. They had to show themselves to a man they didn't want to see, but in the end they didn't really risk anything to get what they wanted.

If I rip you off, you get to comment below my advert and pick how many stars you give me. Twelve jobs now and no one has commented below my advert. Just twelve sets of five stars from twelve happy customers and not one mention anywhere of what was ordered, what went down, what came to a terrible end.

I do think sometimes, though, that no one really wants to piss off a man who does murder for a day job. And how no one now wants to break that five star chain, to be the one client I remember. Our details are unknown to each other, but still no one wants to play games with a gruesome death hidden around some future corner.

My phone in my hand, I stop at the door of a big pub before heading to my hotel. The thick, rich din of indoors is behind me, the thin, wild shouts of the outside are in front. The bladed edge of the language, of even that Bavarian-accented laughter, slices the air all around.

The thing is, though, this is different, isn't it? The thing is, this time I don't know how much I am being watched. The thing is, this is the first time I have done this in the knowledge that there are people outside of myself and the client who know what I do, who may even know where I am right now.

I've taken all the precautions I can take, done all the ducks and dives I can do. We'll just have to see if I ever hear from Imelda or Martin again, and if I do I've a feeling they'll update me on my business.

I sway a little, act a little pissed now as a king-size barmaid comes my way, her arse so full-on it's visible from the front, her strong hands gripping steins of slopping beer. I take her picture as she offers me one.

Risk assessment?

I don't have a department for that. I don't have a fact collector, an up-to-the-minute researcher.

Risk assessment?

Does it count that an old Russian contact helped me make sure I bounce myself and my emails around the online world leaving no trace at all?

Risk assessment?

I'll take my chances. I do what I can, but, as for the rest of it, I'll take my chances. Risk assessment can cause overconfidence, an overreliance on circumstances that were assessed when they were not in front of your face, and I figure that can be a bad thing.

Risk assessment?

No risk assessment would have told me that someone, some-where, knows who put that 'hard solve' advert up. No assessment would have stopped Imelda and Martin getting to me, by whatever craft and guile they used.

No assessment tells me right now that they pose a danger, that I should already be running. My gut is telling me not to worry, to go back to where I was. My gut is telling me that they will come back to me, that they wouldn't expect me to stop.

And, anyway, fuck it, I've got my wits about me.

You want to stop me doing this? Come on ahead, put your foot out, trip me up. Come on, stand in my way see how you fare with me as your opponent. You want to see me in court? Come on ahead, roll up all your evidence and send the cops round. You'll find you have got fuck all my friend, fuck all hard evidence. At best there's a non-specific confession made under duress on the streets of Amsterdam, so I wish you good luck.

I take more pictures, make more reasons for being here, start confirming that I will not become a formal suspect for what is about to happen. And I take a big bite out of this beer and start laughing now about being sad about not getting more contact from Imelda, from Martin.

And I'm laughing because my thinking has a different tone, is going into a different mode. I'm laughing and taking off some figurative coat, laughing and tucking my wheels in, taking wing on this strangely life-affirming bloody journey once again tonight.

★

I make up a syringe of heroin in the hotel and pocket it, half a cork on the end, pull on a second-hand tweed jacket and scarf and leave for the Hofbräuhaus.

It's 21:07 and two hundred are drinking at the tables outside, clinking glasses and chugging down full mouths of joy.

My target sits among twenty-three men, all lapping up the ceremony and looking forward to the controlled chaos that lies ahead of them.

There are two gangs here: the German-based Brekkers and the English-based Blue Woolies. Between them, they've seen a thousand dogs die hard in pits, mauled to death, exhausted to the end. They've watched canine flesh get gripped and torn, they've found wild pleasure among high-stake bets and happy cheers, in hours-long fights that end only when one wretched dog is declared dead.

They've ramped up the aggro in their steroid-fuelled hounds, blooding them on countless coiled, shivering pets, on stolen mutts and moggies, on easy prey for drugged beasts with permanent headaches that are taught not to learn or live, but only to stop or destroy.

My target is Roy, thirty-five, a lanky fucking daddy-long-legs of a man, an echo of a man, a pimple of a man. He has form for burglary, for beating up various mothers and lovers, is banned from visiting three of his six hopeless kids. He's Roy, walked free from court with a finger in the air after there wasn't enough to convict him for being what he is. Roy, cash-rich and cruel, head of the Blue Woolies, mocking any system he can leech off, any system he can breech or bankrupt or force to acknowledge his significance.

He's Roy and I see him crack the end of some joke now before he swagger-staggers himself off to the bogs inside, his big, white Nikes failing to do it in a straight line. And I know this is a fine time to hard solve the cunt of a problem that is Roy.

In the bogs, packed with pissing boozers, I get behind him as he looks at himself in the mirror, an inch or two taller than me.

He checks his hair, checks his profile, tells himself with his own face how he is that rare case of a loser winning everything.

Roy sees me smile in the mirror behind him, feels the needle drive into his thigh. His leg pulls to the side, his instinct telling him to get away from me, and I shove him sideways.

By the time he has thought of what he is going to say, he has stopped thinking. My eyes are on his as he crumples up his face, starts to drop.

Roy gets all my support as we leave, my arm around his, pulled straight into a taxi at the rank outside. None of Roy's guys see a thing as I throw his legs in after him, close his door, get in the other side and tell the taxi man to drive.

'Eurobizpark, *bitte*.'

I chat in German all the way, explaining we're brothers from Scotland, how we were born in Bavaria, how we are Bavarian before we are German, German before we are Scottish, how we love to come back every year for Oktoberfest, and he's heard too many drunk bastards saying shit like this to be arsed saying much at all.

We're out at the centre of Eurobizpark, an area full of shiny box units, a place that is hollow to the core when there's no one around. I put Roy over a shoulder as the taxi disappears, carry him to the lock-up where the fights are due to happen tonight.

I drop him on the ground around the back, wrap my scarf around my right hand and punch through the office window. It takes two, three whacks before I can reach in, open it, before I get to climb in.

By now, the dogs are going crazy.

I clamber onto the desk, my one-size-too-small charity-shop boots kicking an ashtray, some newspapers, pens and cards and biscuits onto the floor. I use the scarf to pull open drawers, to knock a phone from the wall, to toss over a lamp, a table, some weird fantasy ornament that can only be Angela Merkel in the nude.

I walk from the office into the main unit floor, the snarling and barking now at live-orchestra level, but visceral, hellish. I pull smacked-out, groaning Roy in through the back door and pull it closed.

The floor is in sections, 100 square metres, multi-purpose, cutting-edge. They've made a pit in the centre, lifting out the lightweight half-metre-square, easy-clean blocks to build a ten-metre by ten metre hole for the dogs to fight in.

On one side of the unit, each with a curtain draped over its cage, are the dogs. Sixteen of them chained up inside sixteen pens, all hungry and angry and hurting from slamming sore, filed-sharp teeth into steel bars.

On another side, a wooden crate, delivered for the occasion, with maybe a dozen swiped cats inside. The roaring dogs have silenced them all, and a look through the slats shows the creatures gathered together, in one quivering, defensive, clawed ball of terror.

I walk in front of the dogs, lifting each curtain in turn, a quick look to get an idea of its ferocity. I pick the meanest, most tragic looking animal, whip the curtain off, let it dance insanely, bashing its head and fangs off the cage, slavering as it watches me, demented by its training, by its desire only to kill.

I place my mobile on top of the cage, start up a downloaded, a generic recording of cats meowing, sending their infuriating, unmistakeable squeals into the personal space of this bursting, searing Staffordshire pit bull.

I haul long Roy up over my shoulder again, flip open the lid of the cat crate and look down at the hissing felines, at the beloved pets of people whose most distressing fears are being realised.

Roy is lowered in, head first, and right away the cats scrab and scratch, swipe and scrape and tear at his face. He is barely with us but as his eyes and lips lacerate and bleed, as the cuts multiply on his face, he is reacting, pulling, blinking, somehow now acknowledging what is happening.

I let him spill in further, folding his neck on the floor of the wooden box, his hair, clothes and skin now sucking up the scent of terrified moggies, their spittle, their piss, their blood.

And out comes Roy, my back aching now, and I'm thankful I have just one more place to put him. I pull the crate, tipping it over, leaving a wide open door for the cats to run for their lives.

They give it a few seconds, as I'm dragging Roy away, before they begin bolting out of their jail, dashing as far as they can from the dogs, searching for an exit.

I pull bloody-faced Roy to the pit, drop him down, kick him in, hear him give some kind of yelp as he lands on his side, his own blood smeared across his junk-fed face.

I walk to the cage, unhook the lock, watch as the mad dog bounces with furious savagery, its neck almost tearing its chain apart. I climb on top of its pen, detach the chain, feel the animal pull hard away from me, feel its tugging rage and the cage shaking as it senses prey, blood, death.

I drop down behind it, let it lead me to Roy, sniffing and snarling, barking insanely as it learns, with each step, more and more about the stinking, silent, still creature in the hole. I put my foot on its arse, just in case it needs any help, and push it into the pit.

As they say, the fight is won before you get in the ring.

The other dogs rampage around their pens at the sound of an attack underway. I collect my phone from the cage, cut the cat noises, film the footage I might need of Roy being pulled by his ear, by his head, hands, from one side of the pit to the other.

I film as the brick-shithouse, bulging-eyed dog goes for his face, as Roy gasps, throws an arm up in some kind of protest. It goes for his neck as Roy, high as fuck on heroin, confused beyond what his brain can take, kicks out at the uncontrollable viciousness tearing biscuit-sized chunks of flesh from his body.

I wait for as long as I must, checking the front door, checking the back door, not knowing when the fight fans will show. I watch as the beast locks onto Roy's jawbone, pulls him again around the pit, painting the floor with thick, broad trails. I watch as it instinctively returns to his neck, sinking into it, easily crushing it. I calculate he cannot survive this, that he will depart sooner than I had expected – and on it goes, on and on it goes.

I stop filming, put the phone away, pace to the back door, check the window, open the door wide, leave it that way. Cats begin, one by one, to exit at bullet speed all around me.

It won't be long, I reckon, before a fast decision is made to clear that red mess up, to mop up what has happened here.

Chapter Twelve

November 2016

I AM sitting at the *Sunflowers* and I hear a woman's heels snap across the floor in a sort of inappropriate asymmetric beat, a rhythm that suggests the wearer is limping.

As she sits beside me, the faint scent of a recent glass of white wine arriving at the same time, I am willing to bet a limb it's Imelda.

Three months since her last communication and she flies – I'm assuming – from Dublin, so that she can sit beside me.

'Well done, Aloysius,' she says, and I can smell some out-of-season winter fragrance, some scent she is declaring herself with, some layer to hide the booze and long morning.

'How so?'

'Well done,' she says, 'with your stealth.'

Her accent lengthens that last word, tapers its ending silently down into the thoughtful quietness of the Van Gogh museum.

'My stealth?'

'You totally dropped off the radar. And soon after, funnily

enough, Roy Bickerstaff dies in a very terrible dog-related accident.'

'Never heard of him.'

'And when I say terrible . . . '

'Never heard of him.'

'I mean terrible. They found him with no face in the boot of a Volvo at a scrap merchant's. His mates did it, the German coppers reckon. But the mates are claiming they were just trying to hide him because he would draw too much attention. I'm hearing, Aloysius, they're claiming someone drugged Roy and dragged him to a pit, set an eight stone pit bull on him.'

I say, 'They would say that wouldn't they?'

I look at her and she is looking at the *Sunflowers*, coat bundled beside her on the bench, laptop bag over her shoulder. Her hair is freshly dyed, a fuller silver, all pulled back tight over her head, all showing the rich maturity of her face, the tough beauty of her blossomed skin under the lights above. Those glowing blue eyes turn to me and she shakes her head.

'I reckon,' she says, 'and it's a mad reckoning – but I reckon you went to Munich on a bicycle.'

I turn back to the blooms, think how there are other versions of these scuffed masterpieces, all by the master's own shaky hand, scattered all over the world. None of them are the same as the one I am looking at right now.

She goes, 'You cycled all the way to Munich, left us running around airports wondering where you were.'

She goes, 'Tell me Aloysius, did you actually go on a bicycle? I can't work it any other way in my head. Did you cycle five hundred and whatever miles – and back – on a fucking bicycle?'

I shrug.

She shakes her head, goes, '*Unglaublich.*'

I shrug.

'Unbelievable', she says, and she can believe what she wants.

She looks around her, looks back at me, goes, 'It'll keep you fit anyway, this lifestyle of yours. You certainly do have the pulse of health about you.'

And I too had noticed it had been good for me, that the journey had toned me up and got the engine – the heart, lungs, system – relishing the pace, enjoying the workout. I too had considered how nobody notices a man on a bicycle, and that he's a tricky thing to follow from the skies over the pedal metropolis of Amsterdam.

I go, 'What happened to your leg?'

'Eh?'

'You're limping.'

She goes, 'I just can't walk so well in these bloody heels after a few hours.'

'Why bother with them then?'

'Whatever,' she says.

'Why wear those heels if they don't suit you, as a person?' I say.

'Whatever,' she says. 'Just to confirm, you are of course not a suspect in anything, Aloysius, so I don't need to say any more about Munich.'

'I know that,' I say. 'You should ditch the shoes though.'

'Okay,' she goes, 'okay, fuck's sake. I stubbed a toe as well, which explains the limp.'

'What did you stub it on?'

'On three hours of sleep and five or six gin and tonics.'

'Painful?'

She goes, 'Tell me, are you depressed? Is that why you come here? To wallow in your depression? You and Van Gogh, brothers in misery?'

And I'm thinking how she's maybe on to something there, that I come here to go low, to deep dive to where it's quiet and still, to do some kind of hiding.

I bring my complete lack of knowledge about what I'm looking at here and try to get lost in among it. I come here on mornings when I've found myself cleaning my teeth for that little bit longer, when I've been filling holes in my mind with other people's days, other people's ages.

I turn to her, 'Have dinner with me tonight.'

She says, 'I will.'

★

We go Indonesian. She's in navy blue with those same heels and hasn't changed her hair and looks close to beautiful when we meet. I don't know what to say and she doesn't say anything as the waiter settles us at the table.

She looks up, as if about to declare an interest in what to have, and says, '*Fingerspitzengefühl.*'

I go, 'Sorry?'

She goes, 'You heard. It's a – how best to put it in English? – it's a lightness of touch, a way of dealing with things, of getting necessary things done in the best, smartest way. Situational awareness, emotional intelligence. You have it in spades, Aloysius.'

'I do?'

'You do,' she says, scanning the menu, 'but you know that anyway.'

'Know that I have it in spades?'

'No. You know the word – *fingerspitzengefühl.* Sure you're fluent in German.'

'I am?'

'Yes. And Dutch. And French. Your Russian's not bad either. A smattering of Hebrew and Arabic as well. And, funnily enough, your Irish is perfect.'

I go, 'Imelda . . . '

She goes, 'Shhh. I want you to stop lying now, Aloysius. I want you to stop it.'

And she's shaking her head, her face telling me as sincerely as it can that she no longer wants to deal with the outside, that she really does want to get to the inside.

I look back to the menu and say, 'It's your turn. You're going to be doing the talking tonight. That's why we're here.'

She goes, 'No problem at all. I plan to be an open book, no problem at all.'

And I don't believe her.

She says, 'You're annoyed that we put all that work into getting you and then, apparently, just let you go. Isn't that right?'

Whatever.

She goes, 'But we didn't do that at all. I was waiting. I had to wait for Munich to happen. I wanted to see what you would do. You needed to get back to work yet you knew my eyes were all over you.'

'I hope you enjoyed losing track,' I say.

'I did, but only for the right reasons.'

'Whatever,' I say, 'it's done now. No more talking about it. Some things have a natural end, Imelda, even if you can't see that.'

'And some things have a time when they should begin,' she says.

She tells me I was ditched as a newborn, found in the woods off a tree-lined road in Tempo, County Fermanagh, in 1976. She says the belief is that one of two men could be my father, and that one of those men died in an Irish border gunfight between soldiers and the IRA. We eat as she tells me I was fostered by nuns, handed over for schooling to a priest-run and now infamous state institution in County Louth aged three, that I faced abuse until I was sixteen. At some stage I headed to Dublin, then London and, at twenty-three, was known to be working in campsites on the south coast of France, cleaning bathrooms, cutting grass, screwing tourists and getting high.

'There are a few blanks,' she says, 'but we have you mingling with French-Algerians in Marseilles, doing some security work, a bit of door work, in and around the city at that time. In the '90s we have you doing some mercenary work in the Balkans, a couple of big paydays for a few jobs, some undercover stuff that no Western government wanted to touch. That bled – we understand – into some paid time with the Chechens, which ended when you were taken by the Russians and given what the Americans think was a spell in prison. I can't imagine that was very nice. We don't know what went on, but we do know you somehow got a claw hammer smashed into your right knee. Luckily you were given a new state-of-art ceramic-and-titanium knee by the Ruskies and it seems to work very well. To the best of our knowledge you made your own way back through Europe, just like any backpacker would, but stopping off in Israel, Gaza and Spain. You taught English in Barcelona for a time, and worked your way back to Ireland. That's when your case came up, the fact that you did not have an Irish passport.

'Our friend Martin, who was at the time taking an interest in people such as yourself at the Department of Foreign Affairs, got you all fixed up. Funny thing is, we understand you never had a passport of any kind, which leaves me baffled as to how you did all that travelling. Can you shed any light?'

I say, 'None at all.'

She goes, 'For eighteen years, Aloysius, you were pretty much invisible. You went dark, dropped off the radar. Do you know how rare that is?'

I say, 'No.'

She goes, 'For the guts of a whole generation, your life is a closed book. What I do know is that, evidently, you are well-trained in mind and body, and that you get stuck in and thrive, sometimes creatively, in adversity. To add to that, right now you're a very highly rated fucking assassin who has still never once – not even once – been questioned by police. And you wonder, dear Aloysius, why I am interested in you?'

I say, 'I just travelled, just walked and worked and did my thing. I didn't have a home to go to. Don't read too much into any of it.'

She stares, shrugs, says, 'This is great food, isn't it?'

I say, 'Yes.'

She calls the waiter. We order desert, more wine, and sit in a strangely comfortable silence.

'You're up next, soldier,' she says, drinking. 'Fire away with whatever it is you want to say.'

I go, 'You want me to work for your agency.'

'Yes.'

'Which, on behalf of some kind of forces, whether inside or very close to the Irish government, wants some people dead.'

'Yes.'

Immediately I like her bluntness, her answers to my statements.

I say, 'You want me to kill Irish people for the Irish government.'

'Yes.'

'Who?'

'Can't tell you.'

'How many?'

'Four.'

'And then?'

'Then that's it.'

'Bollocks.'

She looks up, 'Bollocks? Not sure I understand what you mean there, Aloysius.'

'I'd be a bit of a loose end, don't you think?'

She goes, 'Ah, this paranoia again. You think I would want you to work for me and then I would have you dispatched? Is that what you're saying to me?'

'Yes. Makes sense. I'd know too much.'

'I would also know too much. And no one is planning on killing me, are they?'

'I don't know.'

'They're not. And what, for example, if your country needed your services again and you were dead in a ditch?'

We eat.

'Why me?'

'Seriously? You still want me to answer that?'

'Yes. Is it just because I'm hard to find, that I get lost easy?'

'It's more than that. It's because you barely exist. Because your moral code is fucking haywire, if there even is one. Because I simply don't have to spend the next year telling you that for the greater good some people have to die because you already know about how this stuff works. Because, Aloysius, you are pre-trained, ready for action. Because you have killed before in Christ knows how many situations. Because in the last two years alone you have killed thirteen people and – if your ratings system is to be believed – no one has as much as looked at you.'

I say, 'Where do you get your information? And don't tell me it's your own. Don't tell me it's Dublin. The network just isn't big enough. The budgets aren't big enough.'

She licks around her teeth.

'The Americans,' she says. 'Martin has some sort of ask-no-questions thing going on, been that way for years. Don't ask me about it.'

I say, 'I'm asking.'

She goes, 'When they need help looking at Brits, at French people, Irish people, whatever, we know people in Ireland who will sort it out for them, for the Americans. We can get ridiculously close in   situations where they can't even get onto the same street. The Americans are expected, we are not. In turn, if we need some background on a person of interest out there somewhere distant in the world, they will get that for us. They can see most things, find out a lot of stuff. Yes, you went dark out there, but we got quite a bit on your past. They make great friends, the Americans, but terrible enemies. So, as I said, Martin sorts it all out. He's a genius at that stuff. He does all those Irish-American handshakes, you know. He works that whole Celtic diaspora thing and I can tell you it goes a long way.'

I go, 'Do the Americans know what you want me for? Why you're looking at me?'

She shakes her head. 'No. They wouldn't care anyway. Doesn't affect them, keeps us all friends. They'd just look the other way on a case like this. Just don't kill any Yanks, basically. Truth is, Aloysius, the CIA see the British as minor rivals. They don't like sharing intelligence or being beaten to anything by the other guy, by the likes of MI6. But they always see us as friends, always in some way useful to them, never a threat to them. All said and done, our relationship is more special with them than anything the Brits have going. It's in our interest to keep it that way.'

I push my plate to her.

She looks at it, looks up.

'One thing bothers me,' she says, 'and I'm just going to say it, right?'

'Right.'

'I'd feel a lot more comfortable if you were a patriot.'

'Now that's a weird thing to say.'

She goes, 'What I do, and what I want to do with you, is for Mother Ireland. These are things to be done, ultimately, for very good reasons: for the greater good of the state, for the Irish people, for the heart of the nation, for the society that lies beyond our own lives. If you were to come on board in the current circumstances, I don't know if I would have a full understanding of your motive.'

She folds her hands, that power move she does. The waiter asks if they'd like anything else. I ask for the bill.

She fixes me, as if telling me she wants me to say it.

'You can't make me go all dewy-eyed Irish on you,' I say. 'You can't just flick a switch, Imelda. That stuff isn't my bag. I don't feel any more at home in Ireland than I do in Holland.'

'That doesn't mean you don't love Ireland.'

'It means I don't want to label or define myself in a way that is convenient to others.'

She smiles.

I go, 'It's hard, you know. It's actually hard not to love your country, your first home, where you first breathed, for better or for worse. It's an opt-out situation, it's a decision you take to move from the default position. And it's a decision I have thought through.'

'Well,' she says, 'decisions can always be reviewed.'

I go to speak and she cuts across.

'I'll pay the bill,' she says, 'if that doesn't define you too much.'

I say, 'To define is to limit.'

She nods. 'Indeed, Aloysius. You know your Wilde.'

And I say, 'Yes, I do.'

★

I'll break your chain letter, answer your door at midnight, jump into any lion's den you can find. I'll enter the scary house, shout at the shouter, run at the suicide bomber, stand in front of the bullet, blade or train.

I'll do these things because, all said and done, I have the measure of my own mind, the understanding of the worth of who I am, the sure knowledge that I'm better off dead by you than damned by you. This mind of mine may have holes in it, but I don't want to fill them with things that have no business being there, things that try to inform every other thought, every other part of me that I have built from nothing and made strong.

Patriotism makes people excited when they put a nationality sticker on the back of their car and take it across Europe.

Patriotism leads to grown men announcing to the world what they are not and cannot be. It announces to the world – like that €5 car sticker – more truly where they're going than where they're from. Patriotism makes grown men homesick. I've seen people live and die for it, for their country, their nationality, their religion, walking around in their mini-environments like spacemen, sucking in their own gas over and over until it weakens and kills them.

I tell Imelda I hated growing up in Ireland, but it was people who tormented me and people I knew of who I hated, not the land mass I stood and knelt on. I tell Imelda that I love Ireland as much as I love anywhere else, that one rock among all the other rocks is not the right place on which to map and build a belief, a cause.

I tell her that she is losing her mind if she wants me to tell her I love Ireland so that she can feel happier about me killing Irish people.

I tell her, dandering our way arm-in-arm through night-time Amsterdam, through the Red Light District and back to her five-star Dam Square hotel, that she is only as Irish I am.

'And,' I say, 'I'm only as Irish as you. How we feel about the place doesn't mean a thing. For such a practical woman, you're a bit of a dreamer. The Irish are no better and no worse than anyone else. They can stoop as low and reach as high as anyone else. We are no braver than anyone else, no more scared than anyone else, no smarter or stronger. Patriotism tells you you're different, that you're special, that you're from a chosen land. It's just a club, a gang, a group, some kind of fake elite, just one of the stupid things we do as humans to help make sense of the world and our place in it. It's just definition, just pattern-making on that globe we look at. All we do as humans is define, chase up patterns so we can box and understand what's around us, to find where we are in it, but we're only talking about words.

'I think it's better to escape that shite, to do what camouflage does, to break up the outline and fuck up the pattern, to break the boundaries and keep going.'

I tell Imelda, 'You say Irish patriotism? I hear gunshots and victims and charity, loss, greed, pain, busted kneecaps and fucking ballads. I see bowing down and standing too tall, I see too many people doing too much of the hard, wrong thing at the wrong time. I see misunderstood moments and misrepresented people. If I listen closely I hear phobias, nationalism, murder and alcohol. I'm not spending my days getting my head around all that. Life's too short.'

She pulls my arm tighter, somehow disarming me, somehow making it seem as if I am saying things that make sense in her mind, as if I am being listened to, and it makes me go quiet.

'I'm surprised you didn't say potatoes,' she says gently, 'or Aran fecking jumpers.'

And I have to tell her that she knows what I mean, but she cuts me off.

'You've been away a long time, Aloysius,' she says. 'You have the thoughts of a second generation. So you do. To be sure. Ye boy ye.'

Fuck it.

She knows what I mean.

I shake my head.

We stroll along the canal-side, among high, happy and horny people, weaving around the shocked and thrilled visitors to the city.

We look in windows that are impossible not to witness, at their pinkish, naughty neons as women in underwear smile and frown and shake at passing guests.

Imelda goes, 'Who did you fight for in Chechnya, Aloysius?'

And she knows she can only play at the edges, that opening one door at a time is enough for now. She knows I won't answer.

She goes, 'Why did the Russians take you from there? Why did they give you a new knee and let you go? And what were you doing in Israel, and on the Gaza strip? Whose side are you on, whose side have you been on? Who have you killed and what for? Whose judgement led to you taking the lives you have taken?'

And I can tell where she's going with this pretty fast.

She says, 'Have you killed because of the hot momentary decision of some tribal leader? Some rich politician? Have you killed because of the whim of a patriot from some other land? Have you killed because of the fury of a father? I ask all that because you seem to have all the answers. I'm asking because I'm sure you can explain the sense behind all it is you have done with your life.

'I'm asking you to tell me what wisdom you have, in all honesty, brought to the world. What is it that makes you better than a little old Irish spud like me, Aloysius?'

And I tell her how I know I am no better, no wiser.

'Well,' she says, 'maybe it's time to start making a pattern, to help the rest of us out. Maybe it's time to pick a team, to get some loyalty into your heart, to try and fill up some of that empty space you so obviously carry around, that swallows you up when you're alone.

'It's a human imperative, Aloysius, to be some identifiable thing, to have a name. Sooner or later you have to make things make sense, find the point to things, label things, whether you like it or not. We give names to all of this structuring we do around us, we call it the work or God or love or some fucking thing. But whatever we call it, you're only a man at the end of the day, and you cannot be anything else.

'Let me tell you, Aloysius, there are much, much worse things in this world than patriotism. Patriotism is kinship, bonding. It forms nations, forges pride and confidence. It is enjoyed by those who demonstrate it, and enjoyed too by those who see it in others.

'I love a patriotic Frenchman and I'd be disappointed to meet one who wasn't. Same with the Greeks, the Italians. I could damn well cry when I hear the American national anthem, when I hear Elvis sing 'Dixie'. I love a Scotsman who sings, drinks and sheds tears for his country, who wears a frigging kilt and beats seven bells of shite out of anyone who slags it off. Tell me what that mad, proud Scotsman is doing wrong? Can you answer me that?'

And she leaves no room for an answer.

'I admire,' she says, 'anyone who can put their hand on their heart and tell me who they are.'

I go, 'Which can too easily become a way of telling you who they are not.'

'Shut the fuck up,' she says. 'You're estranged from yourself, Aloysius, and I find it both a little pathetic and a little offensive.'

And I feel like apologising.

She goes, 'This year, 2016, is the centenary of the Easter Rising, a moment when Ireland was redefined by Irish people. A hundred years ago we found some collective fusion and realised, after those bold, thinking men were dispatched at Kilmainham, that something had to give.

'As a nation, we've put a good display in the window this year but made a balls of truly sorting through the stock in the back of shop. We won't let ourselves talk about the past without talking about its legacy, about the hard politics of it today. Over and over again we are taking it all too literally, living inside what happened, living in narrow facts that none of us saw, and missing the greater power and symbolism of the past. It pisses me off, I can tell you.

'We're on the road to 2021 and '22 now. A hundred years on from the formation of the state. And likewise, it means a lot in a lot of ways.

'I won't believe for a second you don't understand how millions of Irish people will have numbers like those at the fronts of their minds, how they are already discussing what a hundred years on means to our special little green, wet sod. And you choose to bat it all away as if it's for eejits, as if it's not in your blood as much as it's in mine?

'You're lying, but only to yourself. You're no breath of fresh air, Aloysius. You're no new thinker, no mould-breaker, no man who cannot be put in a box.

'You're just a man on the run, just like half the men in the history of our land. Running. Leaving. Clearing out. A Paddy fucking off to find the new, to go and be the cute charmer somewhere else.

'At least most of those who left before you never denied where they came from, at least they had the balls to accept themselves for who they are, to accept the fact that, land mass full of problems or not, it's their fucking land mass, and raise a glass to it.

'This is an important time to be Irish, and all of your theorising and gurning about your own past, whatever violence or rape or mental torture you suffered, won't change any of that.

'It's an important time to be Irish, and a very useful time to get on and do the work I want to do, to give our land reason to pull together, to feel the same thing at the same time. I want to play our country some good mood music at a time when we are wondering what mood to be in.'

And I go, 'How?'

'What would you say,' she says, 'if we were able to remove people from our society who, by any human standards, by any standards at all, had no right to be alive any longer?

'What would you say if I could predict the future, that the unmistakable symbolic power of some real events were destined to help act as a rising tide for Ireland?'

I say, 'I would say that thinking you can play with the future is a very silly business.'

'Why?' she says. 'It's what you do all the time. You change things permanently, don't you? What is the term you use – you "hard solve" things. You hard solve problems and it changes lives, makes people relax, makes people more comfortable in themselves. That's why they hire you, isn't it? That's the end result of what you do, isn't it? People hire you to remove trouble, to brighten their future. My need is no different.'

She goes, 'What do you want the future to hold for a loan shark so selfish and greedy that he left babies hungry as he beat and raped their mothers, year after year after year?

'Or what do you want for a paedophile who destroyed thousands of young lives, who is now planning to publish every name and detail from his hellish exploits, yet still has nothing but adoration for himself?

'What do you want for a woman who is planning a bloodbath, who wants to blast open deep, sore wounds that are only just healing, north of the border?

'What would you say to all that? Maybe you don't even know. But I know what 99-percent of Irish people will say – they'll say "*slán*" – "good fucking riddance" – "happy fucking days".'

'And what a time it would be to say it, after this land has been battered and abused and tricked for decades, battered and abused and robbed from within to the point where people like you have turned their back.

'What a time to show a few chapters physically closing, to get out and add some welcome schadenfreude to this period of our history.

'What a time to say "out with the old and in with the new". What a time to begin again, to capture and lift the national heart. The ends would justify the means, would they not?

'What if we were to do this, to succeed, to create a cluster of good luck, to give people a foothold towards a bright new century? What if it all came at a time when there's a re-emerging buoyancy in the fortunes of the state, a fresh synergy at a time when we are looking to tell the world who we are, to tell ourselves who we are?'

I laugh at that.

'And who are we?' I say. 'All sons and daughters of 1916? It's that simple to you, is it? Is that where you want all this to go? For everyone to look back and go "Those were the days"? We're more than that, different than that. Not all the blood in Ireland runs green, Imelda. You maybe don't see it from your locked-tight Dublin office but there are people north of you whose instincts work differently, who would be traitors to themselves, to their loved ones, to their country, to the blood they've shed, if they were to magically fit in with your idea of who they should be, of what you think should make them tick. That's part of your problem, you see, you can't understand how identity works, just how deep it goes, until it gets challenged.'

She goes, 'I'm talking about enhancing the good stuff, getting shot of the bad. I'm telling you I want anyone who feels so inclined to feel positive about who they are, not who they are not. I'm talking about spirit and courage, about independence and leadership, not about venom and anger and division. I can't change Northern Ireland any more than anyone else, and I don't even think I'd want to – there's nothing in the world wrong with passion and identity.

'It's the Ireland of saints and scholars that I believe in, Aloysius, not the land of shameless soldiers who have their hands out for the dole in between breaking kneecaps and making fucking nail bombs.

'Those ballads you talked about, they work when they tell the truth. You can wrap sentiment around any old bastard, but good luck to you if you think we'll all sing along.

'This is a young little nation and, like any youth, it needs a little bit of guidance, a bit of a push onto the next level, to a place where it can know itself better.

'If you come on board with me, that will be your job, and Martin's, and mine. If you're not proud of your country, you can help now by changing it. You can help by making the sort of changes for the future that only a man like you can make.

'What's there to lose? A few fucking scumbags? I don't care about that, do you? Even if we fail, we win. Even if we fail we'll know ourselves that bit better, and there is nothing more useful than that. Even if we fail, we "fail better", as Samuel Beckett would say, than we've failed before.

'So what do you think? You've done this kind of thing in the past for Jesus knows who. But this time, this special time, it's your own country calling.'

And we're stopped, looking at an angled Asian beauty swaying slowly in a window for all who pass by, nodding now at us, urging us to couple and triple and share each other in any pattern, language or currency. And the heated, simple drive of Imelda's boyish team-talk hangs around my head, the echoes darting chaotically through my mind.

'A hundred years on,' I say, 'and more executions by the state.' And I look at her.

'Yes,' she says, eyeing the model in the window, the external perfection for hire, 'but don't be telling anyone.'

Chapter Thirteen

Russian Military Training Base
Tajikistan, Central Asia

December 2007
Evaluation Interview #19

'IT'S TEMPTING to fill in the gaps. That's how we got God, that's how we got scared of the dark, that's why we wonder. But sometimes that's all you can do – wonder – because you know that no answer is ever going to come.

'One time this nun told me she'd heard on the grapevine that my dad was a British soldier, worked with the Ulster Defence Regiment, a hard-nosed crew whose job was to take on the IRA.

'This nun heard he was from Belfast, that he was serving in County Fermanagh in 1975 or '76. He had a rank one or two above a private soldier and was a difficult man to work with.

'They sent him to Fermanagh to lead a crackdown on some IRA unit that were having it all their own way, that had attacked and killed police and soldiers, terrorised some farmers out of the area, and were making it known that this was a no-go area for anyone who didn't back them.

'This nun said the solider had his men pop up on certain roads all the time, stopping cars all the time, frustrating IRA operations, showing that they were also controlling ground. She said he had his men grilling people about who or what they knew, even if they knew nothing, even if they knew so much they wouldn't say a word. He wanted word spread around that he was mean and meant business and he very quickly became the IRA's big target there.

'He used to drink too much, could be a bit loose with his security, she said. He ended up knocking them back in some pub in Enniskillen one Saturday night, got recognised by this woman, this woman who was the girlfriend of some way up guy in the local IRA. She couldn't get in touch with her boyfriend at the time, but didn't want to let this man out of her sight. So she moved in, started chatting, flirted with him, honey-trapped him into coming with her, into telling no one where he was going.

'He was so horned-up and pissed that he went along with it. She got behind the wheel of his car, with him singing in the passenger seat, and drove to her boyfriend's house in this village called Tempo, about ten miles away.

'The pair of them went in and, when he was settling down, she put a call in to some pubs, tried again to round up her fella, to get him home with a few IRA players to interrogate, and finish this man on their own turf.

'But all the guys she knew were out all over the town, all drinking, and everything just started to take too long. It was getting too uncomfortable having this man she wanted dead sitting around in her house, but she had to go with it, had to interact.

'She spent some more time with him, chatting and canoodling, doing whatever to kill the time, but she was always still hoping that her boyfriend would just pull into the yard. He was at a level in the IRA where he could call a kill or lead an interrogation any time he wanted, and she needed him to come and claim this big target she had sitting there for him.

'It was about two hours before she lost it, before she'd had enough. She was getting to the stage where she was making friends with this man she wanted to kill and she didn't like it, where the division between them was being breached, where he was becoming harder to kill. She knew she had to take action on that, had to just sort this out for herself.

'So she went and got a hammer, went back into the room, and he was standing there, sober as a judge, camera in his hand, taking pictures of the room around him.

'He was saying to her, "Now you see honey, that's how easy it is."

'He told her he had turned the trap on her, that she was going to be in big trouble with her husband for letting him into that house, that he wanted word to get out that he was the man who could go and do what he wanted, not her boyfriend.

'The guy pretty much left it at that, took some more pictures around the house, took a picture of her, walked out, drove away, left her standing there with the hammer in her hand, halfway to killing someone.

'This nun said the soldier and the woman never spoke again. She said the woman never told her husband what had happened that night, what an error she had made that night, but knew it would come back to haunt her one day.

'Months later, there was a shooting, bullets flying between the IRA and soldiers. The IRA had been on a night-time mission but were ambushed by the UDR and both sides opened up. All of the

IRA unit died, including the boyfriend of the woman who tricked the soldier. And the soldier who tricked the woman was one of the guys who was doing the shooting that night.

'This nun said that woman always knew in her heart it was the soldier who shot her boyfriend. And that was the end of the world for her. She blamed herself, felt she had somehow weakened everything, had let her people down, had been deceiving everyone for too long.

'My part in the story is pretty simple, if you want to believe it. My part is that she waited for a few more months, grieved for a few more months until her baby was born, until I was born, two days before I was expected.

'She had waited to get the thing out of her because it was the thing that started life inside her as she waited for her boyfriend to come home, as she waited for that soldier to die.

'Now I don't know what the story is with that and I don't know if anyone does. This nun told me that the woman believed I was the soldier's child but that I could have been her boyfriend's child too, and that no one really knew.

'This nun said no one knew for sure if she really did sleep with the soldier that night or if the soldier took it on himself to sleep with her whether she liked it or not. No one ever knew what it was that happened in the heat of the mad war situation.

'But this nun reckoned I should know I may have been conceived, somehow, some way, in the middle of some bluffing game, in the middle of two lies being told by two opposites.

'My mother, this nun said, gave birth to me all alone in that house. She said my mother wrapped me up in a blanket and put me in this wee plastic crate they used to carry bottles of milk in.

'That same March evening she took me to this really beautiful part of the road on the way out of wee Tempo, just where the strong trees rise up on both sides and lean over and meet in a canopy at the top. It's this shaded place, some woods on one side, and she took me there in my wee basket and left me. She left me close enough to the little stream so I could hear it flurrying along.

'I went there once, just the once, just as I was leaving Ireland when I was seventeen. It's a place where nature is just doing its amazing thing, where if you stop to take it in you realise that there is struggle and beauty everywhere, in everything.

'You breathe the air under those trees, and it's like the most natural place you could be. The story is that my mother did the most unnatural thing in the world in the most natural place. The story is that I was like some little unloved lump of tot left out under the branches for the next person to find. And I was found, right there, by accident, a few hours later, all bundled up and gurning and crying in that milk crate.

'They found her a couple of miles away. She had wandered through the trees, into the fields, traced the path of the river for a while in her bare feet. Then she just walked into it, let the water go over her head, and never had a plan to come out again.

'I tried to look it all up once, just the once. And there had been a shooting, there had been people killed. There was a story that a certain soldier had been the IRA's main target on the night, that he had left the UDR a few years later and moved to Portugal. But I don't know. Maybe one day I'll check it all out.

'I don't think it's good to go back, to be honest. I think it's good to keep moving, not to stop. I mean, if I ever was to track down that soldier, I'd be tracking down someone who is either my father or the man who killed my father, and I don't know how to feel about a man like that.

'You have to look forward, don't you? Not backward, forward. The mind's eye must point forward or you will not get your journey done.

'I've been training here for six months now for this job in Israel, for "Operation Dante", and I don't think I'll live through it.

'I know now that nothing will get in my way to get it done, but I don't believe the extraction will work. Being here has taught me that I know for sure there is no challenge I will face when I get there that can stop me trying.

'I'm not saying I won't feel fear when I go to do this, it's just that I know what to do with fear, I know not to let it disable me. It's not that I won't cry or worry or feel the world closing in on me because of what I have done in the past, because of what I will do again.

'It's just that when I feel fear, I know I can take it, roll it up in a ball and carry it with me, not as part of me but with me. I can bring it on the journey, feel it like it's a little living thing, a little puppy, and I can take it to the precise place that makes it kick out and snap the most.

'I have learned that I will not bet against myself. I will never bet against myself.

'I've been thinking a lot lately about that priest we talked about before, about Father Barry. I've been thinking how I was the first person to show him how fear could be turned around. If I learned anything from him it was that I had courage somewhere inside, the kind of courage that could take hold of me, could take over a room.

'I got off the floor in his study that last time he hit me and reached for his hand, and he let me take it. I took his little finger and folded it back, pressed on the nail as hard as I could and brought him all the way to the ground.

'He felt it when my cold, bare toes hit him in the face. He felt it when I smashed his brains out and across that floor with a golden Jesus. I was eleven years old.

'The last thing he ever saw was me not being afraid, me taking on the power of his authority, of his strength. The last thing he ever heard was me saying a little Latin phrase I picked up.

'I bashed that bastard and said, "*Nihil timendum est*".

'I told that bastard, "Fear nothing".'

Chapter Fourteen

November 2016

I WAKE up feeling like one of those people who wakes up with a new accent, or with a stranger in their bed, or in a place they can't remember going to.

The beep of the horns outside interrupts my thinking and I'm not going to suffer it. I pack a bag – the bag – and clean what I need to clean from the flat. A farewell double beep sounds my departure as I walk out of the door, down the stairs and into the city.

I call Tall Marianne as I walk, tell her I'm sorry I haven't been in touch, tell her I have some news and hope to meet. She's on Damrak, she says, and we can rendezvous for coffee.

I see her – pouting, a red beret, two inch nails – sitting with a short, wiry guy when I walk into the café. She introduces him as 'Karson with a "K"', and says it's good to hear from me.

'We've been together for a while,' she tells me.

'That's right,' says Karson, beaming, turning a little spoon around in his fingers.

'He's an all-American boy,' she says, 'doing some big work with the university.'

Karson drops his head, his foot tapping and that spoon spinning, looks up and winks at her.

I tell him I've heard the university is great, but what I'm thinking is that his being here is slowing me down and I need to get a move on.

I say to Tall Marianne, 'Things have been crazy this last wee while. Basically I'm leaving town.'

What I'm telling her – and we never speak directly about it – is that I don't need her to hide SIM cards, to leave a vase in the window, to get in touch if she ever feels suspicious about anyone, anything. But I need to ask her something, something I need to ask her alone.

She stands, nodding and unmoved at my words, tells me to sit tight, that she's going to the bathroom.

I fix Karson with a look, a face that tells him I'm wondering who the hell he is. I know, whether on behalf of the Irish or not, there's American eyes and ears all over me. And I feel like some kind of racist, suspicious about him and his American eyes and ears. I am suddenly somehow sitting at a table with an unknown American and, at this moment, it instinctively feels wrong.

Doing some big work with the university.

What the hell does that mean?

I have no idea how to ask someone if they're in the CIA and, even if Karson did have that honour, he would never answer it. So I fix him with that look, let him make what he wants of it. I figure if he is some kind of spy he will be thinking about it right now, and I watch his body language carefully, look for leaks, for signs that he is drawing on training.

And he's busy but confident enough, fairly smiley, a hard-built bijou man, a little tree stump of a man inside all those sinews. I outrank him in age, he's thirty-seven. I outrank him in strength, probably in experience. Yet he has a determination about the way he spends himself.

He doesn't fix me back with any kind of look, just ticks over, moving limbs and fingers and turning his head here and there, getting rid of that nervous energy crackling inside.

I say, 'Not like Tall Marianne to keep a partner for any length of time.'

'No? Oh, that makes me feel good, man,' he says, and he laughs, somehow relieved at the silence breaking.

'How did you meet?'

'Through my work. I was introduced to her at some crazy Amsterdam party. You know the kind of thing.'

I nod, smile, look around, look back. 'What is it you do at the university, Karson?'

'Comms,' he says, 'communications. I help analyse signals, basically. It's kind of high-tech stuff. It's part of an exchange pro-gramme between Washington and the Dutch. What do you do?'

I go, 'I travel a bit, do some photography. From what you're saying, it sounds like you're a spy.'

He nods, 'Yeah, I guess it does. Not a good one though. A real spy wouldn't be so open.'

He's rich, or from a rich family. Maybe has been in some hard-to-enter college fraternity, maybe spun a little too far off the rings from time to time.

And I can't get shot of the idea that he knows everything about me. I'm thinking how the Americans did get close to Marianne, in the end. I'm thinking how Imelda knew her most intimate details before they chased me around the city that day.

And now I'm retelling myself that even if Karson were a spy, he would be friendly, he would have only been spying for the Irish as a favour. That's the story I've been told, and I've no reason to doubt it, do I?

Now I'm telling myself I'm jumping the gun about him, I'm telling myself I'm just too damn jumpy today because I've started a process of opening up and my instincts are scolding me.

I say, 'Excuse me,' and catch Tall Marianne as she's exiting the bogs, fixing her hair, saying 'prune' to herself in a mirror and watching what it does to her face.

She's been my best pal in this city, a girl-about-town hedonist who shuns all codes but loyalty to friends. She's old money Amsterdam, has links to the royal family, is a generous contact and unpaid fixer to half-shadowed figures she meets at parties or gets introduced to at orgies, protests against any authority of any kind.

Ask me who I trust most in the world, even right now, and I'll tell you it's this crazy woman in front of me.

'Listen,' I say, the sum of the security of her friendship at the front of mind now. 'You don't have to do any shit for me ever again, and I thank you for all you have done.'

She shrugs. 'It's nothing. You're a cloak-and-dagger guy. I know the type. I like the type. What I don't know can't hurt me, right? Maybe you'll do me a favour one day.'

I nod, 'I'd be happy to. But the thing is I'm leaving town, okay? As in leaving. You probably won't see me again.'

She's stunned. 'Jeez, aren't you all drama today?'

I look over at Karson as Karson looks over at us, looks like he's trying not to bite his nails.

I go, 'You sure about that guy? He's into you? Not just trying to use you to . . . ?'

'Hey Aloysius,' she goes, 'go fuck yourself. You think a chick with a dick can't have a serious boyfriend?'

'No,' I say, 'wise up. I'm just wary. Cloak-and-dagger mentality. I'd like to know you're safe, that you're not going to get hurt.'

'Karson's a good guy. And I can look after myself.'

'I know that. I know . . . '

'Go,' she says, 'leave Amsterdam. Go to wherever it is you go. Go hide your SIM cards somewhere else, find some other safe house, some other secret messenger. We'll meet again sometime.'

'One thing,' I say. 'One last bit of help.'

'What?'

'Your mum,' I say. 'When she died, she left you the barge. You said there was a car too, a wee car somewhere.'

'Yeah, I've never seen it. Never will see it.'

I push some cash into her hand. She looks down, surprised. 'What?' she says, 'you want the car?'

'Yep. Where is it?'

She pushes the money back. 'Take it. Keep it. It's underground, Oud-Zuid Apartments. Don't ask me where the keys are.'

'I'll find it. What type is it?'

She shrugs. 'A dusty one.'

★

I walk a mile to the address, go into the lobby, drop down a floor to the car park.

Ten motors in here, one of them sad and lonely, a Renault Clio with low tyres, a dusty screen and an out-of-date parking disc.

I check for cameras, check the car's security, smash open the back off-side window, flip open the front door, get on board. I pull the wires, confident I can hotwire this thing in seconds but, naturally enough, the battery is dead as Hector.

'Balls.'

I sit back, close my eyes, run the details of what I'm doing around my mind, try to find another way through this. And I try to find out, from myself, if I'm sure I know what the fuck I'm doing.

Am I too paranoid about that Karson guy? Did I freak him out, freak Tall Marianne out? What are the rules of engagement for a guy on his own, trying to make sure the coast is clear to move when he's sucking drones in above him?

A man in a baseball cap walks into the garage, unsure of his surroundings. Jeans, black sweater. He runs his eyes over the cars, looking for someone, looking for me. I see his face as it swoops past my Clio, the face with the head I busted. He's the bald guy with the boot on my face, the English guy working for Imelda's office. That's Wayne.

He walks a little deeper inside, dipping now, starting to look under the cars, wondering where the hell I went.

This fucker has been following me for I don't know how long – days, weeks, months. It's hard not to take it personally, although fair play to him for doing a good job.

Ex-special forces? Ex-undercover police? He looks the type. But the poor, big bastard has just walked his big boots into my plan and he's not going to walk out of it.

It's funny because Wayne hates me already, hates me with all his heart. That feeling of his is going to go off the scale.

★

We check in at the Port of Roscoff for the overnight sailing. The ignition wire is slack around Wayne's throat, ready for tugging and tying around the headrest if he fucks this up.

I stay low as he opens his passport for the woman in the security box. She waves him through, his black four-by-four slipping into the queue for the ferry to Rosslare.

He eyes me in the mirror and I sit up a little.

He says, 'The Dublin office will definitely be looking for me by now.'

I say, 'I know.'

The line moves onto the ship and I pull up into the front passenger seat, pulling the wire fast from around his throat, making him jump.

I tell him, 'Nothing personal in any of this, Wayne. We're not enemies, not on different sides. I just have to get this shit done my way and can't give you a say, you understand?'

He doesn't answer, just pulls neatly into the few square feet of space we have on this ship they call *Oscar Wilde*.

'It's been long drive,' I say. 'We've eighteen hours ahead of us on this bus. Let's just get some sleep and, I promise you, you're a free man when we get to Ireland.'

He turns to me, a look that gives nothing away.

I go, 'I'll be sure to tell them your neck was on the line the whole way. That's why you didn't contact. That do it?'

His lip curls, his head shakes and his heart pumps with hatred for me.

'Yes,' he says.

We leave it at that.

His mobile is already gone, fucked onto the roof of a parked plumber's van in Amsterdam. He could always make a phone call from the ship, but what for? To what end?

I reckon he'll do fuck all beyond grumble, sink a pint, lie down. And if things go the wrong way for me, I'll dump him overboard, or he'll dump me overboard for trying. One way or another, that would fix it.

We climb the stairs among excited children and overwrought folks, get to the bar deck and split. I go to the back, see him heading off to the front.

Twenty minutes later I take a walk, see him sitting, looking at a golden whiskey, contemplating something, managing his emotions. He watches me stroll in and over to him and looks away.

Light shining on his bald head, I see the scars I've left him, the smashes I rained down on him with the edge of a mobile phone. A man in his line of work finds shame easily, and it hurts.

'Fancy another?' I ask, and he doesn't look back.

'Two of whatever he's on,' I say to the barman.

'What do you reckon to Imelda?' I ask, taking the stool beside him. 'She's trying to bring me in to her agency but I don't know a whole lot about it. How's it working out for you?'

'She's just a boss,' he says, puts his eyes front, watches his next whiskey being poured.

'You think she's on the level?'

'I think you're a fucking prick,' he says, turning to me. 'And if she didn't value you so much for whatever the fuck it is she wants you to do, I'd smash your head off this bar right now. Are we clear, Aloysius?'

I go, 'Wow. Jesus. Well then Wayne, why don't you just break a rule then, give it a go? See how far you get?'

He goes, 'Wow. Jesus. Well, I don't know, Aloysius.'

And two Grouse on ice arrive, two baby bottles of lemonade. I can tell he's not going to refuse it and I'm glad.

I say, 'What are you? Ex-special forces, ex-cop?'

He says, 'Let me answer that this way – go fuck yourself.'

I say, 'You too. *Sláinte.*'

And we drink.

I go, 'How's your one-eyed friend?'

'Taken early retirement,' he says. 'How's your Dutch girlfriend's cock?'

'The same.'

And we drink again.

'It's just circumstances,' I say. 'Following me around Amsterdam like a bad smell, what did you expect?'

He turns to me, takes a deep look at my face, goes, 'How would I know? I don't know who the fuck you are. In fact, who the fuck are you?'

I say, 'Let me answer that this way – go fuck yourself.'

He says, 'Christ, you're an annoying bastard.'

And I say, 'I've been called worse.'

He goes, 'That outfit you're still wearing, the one Imelda bought you. It's the only half decent set of clothes you have, isn't it?'

I go, 'Don't worry Wayne, it's all been washed.'

'I picked all that out for you,' he says. 'She sent me into 'Dam to get you some fresh gear, said you had the dress sense of a doughnut.'

I go, 'Jesus, you're my stylist? Wow.'

He goes, 'Fuck off.'

I say, 'So, Wayne, you think I should carry my phone in my top pocket or just leave it stuck in your head?'

Chapter Fifteen

November 2016

I'M IN the passenger seat as Wayne drives the hundred miles from Rosslare to Dublin. I won't say it's a friendly journey, but it's better than the drive from Amsterdam to Roscoff.

He pulls up where I tell him to, on Camden Street, and I'm about to get out.

'You know I've got to call Imelda now,' he says. 'Tell her about this.'

I nod, 'I know.'

'Pretty sure I'll get sacked today,' he says.

I say, 'Wait until the end of the day, then call her. I think you'll be all right.'

He nods, smiles, 'I'll do that.'

'Grand,' I say, reaching out. We shake for one second and he's looking in the mirror, ready to go.

I get a coffee in a crowded, kiosk-size café, look up a few numbers, dial one of them.

A guy answers, '*Irish Mirror* editorial.'

I say, 'I have a story and photograph for you about Imelda Feather. I don't want any money. What's the chances of meeting?'

★

Five hours later and I'm sitting, cross-legged, damp-arsed, in the dead centre of a GAA pitch. Trees border three sides, and dead ahead of me is the back wall of Imelda's office. From where I am, the third floor is framed between the posts.

It takes around seventy minutes – the wind beginning to stir, the light beginning to dip, the rain beginning to moisten the air – before she clocks me, posed like Yoda, where a ball might be.

She stands still at the window before stepping away. I sit my ground, head up, face full-on in her direction.

Imelda reappears with a pair of binoculars and double-checks my ID at close range. I wink and she takes them away from her eyes. I can almost make out her saying some swear word.

If you have never seen a less-than-happy sixty-four-year-old woman in heels march across a GAA pitch, then you should have a look. There comes a point where she will stop, as Imelda is doing, remove her shoes and shout 'fuck sake' at herself. She continues towards me, her hair seemingly alive like snakes throwing themselves around her puckered face, her white blouse throwing shapes in the breeze.

'What in the name of Jesus are you playing at?'

'GAA.'

'I said what are you playing at? You have the attention-seeking behaviour of a six-year-old.'

'Look who's talking.'

'What? I mean – what?!'

I shrug. I'm not sure what I meant by that, but it sounded like it made sense.

She bucks a shoe at me and I have to duck to avoid a heel in the eye.

She goes, 'Why are you testing me, Aloysius? What the bloody hell is going on in that fecking head of yours?'

'Your husband,' I say, looking up at her insulted face, 'he was called Arthur. Lost a load of money, a couple of million, on a property gamble when the market hit the skids.'

She throws up her shoulders, dramatic as she can, goes, 'So fucking what? What's it to you?'

I say, 'He went for a walk into the sea one morning at Malahide, never came out again.'

'Yes,' she says, 'I heard about that, thanks, Aloysius. I know my husband killed himself. What's your point?'

'Ladies View in County Kerry,' I say. 'It's your favourite view in the world.'

Imelda nods. 'And what?' she says.

'Am I right?'

'Yes,' she says, confused. 'Ladies View, yes. What's your point?'

'When you were a journalist, you once met a government minister in his car, you assured him you would not run a story on his affair providing he privately admitted it to you,' I say.

'And then an advert for that very story you were discussing came on the radio then and there.

'In fact, your own voice came on the radio to plug the story in the next day's paper. The man took a heart attack and you had to call the ambulance.'

Imelda nods again, is realising I'm just going to keep talking, going to make this point the way I want to make it.

She drops her other shoe, sits down in front of me on the grass, pulls up and hugs her legs a little against the rising wind, the uneven sprinkles of soft rain.

'You used to drink vodka in your office in secret, until one day you were caught,' I say.

'Your son Liam wanted to be a paratrooper in the British army and you and your husband fought about it to the point where he walked out of the house and never really came back to you.

'You used to screw a very, very senior policeman and a very, very nasty gangster in your days as a crime reporter, that's how you got all those scoops.'

She goes to speak, 'I—'

'Or so they say.'

She says, 'You've been talking to some of the hacks I used to compete with. They were all jealous fuckers, if you want the truth. The cop I was screwing never gave me a story, although his cunnilingus was front-page stuff, I can tell you.'

I say, 'You had a cervical cancer scare when you were forty-four, but it was a misdiagnosis. Your best friend Ellen was accurately diagnosed with pancreatic cancer in the same year. She died.'

Imelda nods, waves a hand, 'Stop,' she says, speaking up now as the wind rises. 'Stop there. Whatever your point is, you've made it. Now explain it.'

I say, 'In six minutes you're going to get a phone call from a journalist. He's had a very strong tip-off that you – a former high-flying media type turned high-flying government recruitment agent and close colleague of the taoiseach and the president – have been smoking a pile of pot. He has seen a picture of you with a large spliff in your hand in an Amsterdam coffee shop. And that picture on the front page will end your career, no matter how deeply unfair that might seem.'

'Ah,' she says, that cold November wind charging over and through the field now. 'You've turned on me, Aloysius. You're ending it all, so.'

She looks down to the grass, quickly adapted, fast resigned to what's coming next. She's shivering now, out on this big pitch, a place of screams and shouts and sporting struggle she usually just sees and hears from a distance.

'I hadn't expected this,' she says, a mellowness in her voice. 'I'd planned for all sorts of twists and turns from you, but not this. Ah well. Fair enough. An error of judgement about you on my part.'

She looks at me, not an angry face, not even a disappointed face. She looks at me and smiles now.

'I'm sorry this has happened,' she says, 'I really am. I think maybe I didn't give that strong mindset of yours enough consideration. Not to worry. Front-page justice and all of that. I've been behind enough of it myself to know the score.'

Just the cold air runs between us now and I can tell the light has dimmed another notch, that the big Dublin day is drawing to a close.

She smiles again, a kind of casually beautiful smile, and I don't know what to do but shrug.

As she goes to stand, to tell me some forever goodbye, I say, 'But they haven't got the picture.'

She stops, dips to the grass again, says, 'Sorry? I don't get you.'

'The snap of you smoking a spliff,' I say. 'They've heard there is one. I might even have shown one to a reporter or two, but they haven't got a copy of it.'

'What are you up to?' she says.

'Someone is going to call you and bluff it out, tell you they have the picture, describe it to you and see if you will confess. You know the deal, Imelda. You've done the same yourself.'

'But,' she says, 'you do know they can't run anything without it because I'll sue the holes off them?'

'Of course I do. They'd have no proof, it's a straightforward libel.'

'Then why . . . ?'

'I want you to feel vulnerable,' I say. 'I want you to feel spied on. I want you to feel as if I might show up anywhere, do anything, that I can change the direction of your day. I want you to feel that I can bring you down. I want you to feel like I do, to feel as if your private world has been cracked open and rifled through.'

'Okay, I get it,' she says, wiping hair from her face, a chill in her voice now. 'I understand. And I'm sorry.'

'And I want you to know this,' I say. 'I need to do something, something significant. I need to fill one of those holes in my soul you talked about, to do something that fits and works with my very own and very fucked up view of the world. What we've been talking about, Imelda . . . '

She says, 'What we've been talking about, in its own very fucked up way, means something to you, doesn't it, Aloysius?'

'Yes.'

'It means you can play a part in making things better, because you understand that it's people, not places that make bad things happen.'

'Yes.'

'Because,' she says, 'you know exactly what I mean when I say a rising tide lifts all boats. You know what I mean when I say the difference between who we are and who we can be lies in taking action.'

'Yes,' I say, and she's really making me smile now. I can hear it, see it, as if a little fire is starting to burn inside her, to warm her up.

'You know,' she says, 'that it's either Mother Nature or mother-fuckers that make the changes in this world, and the first one of those two is seriously slow at getting things done.'

I go, 'Yes.'

'It's the moving parts that make the changes,' she says.

I say, 'You want me to tell you I've crossed a little bridge into some place called patriotism?'

'No,' she says, taking in a deep breath. 'I don't need to hear it. I just want to hear that you know what it is we are talking about when we talk.'

'Okay,' I say. 'If you secretly want to call my commitment patriotism, you go for it.'

'That's maybe what I will do,' she says. 'What do you call your commitment?'

'Purpose,' I say.

She smiles, pulls her arms in tighter as the trees on all sides rustle together.

'Danny Latigan,' she says. 'Started out as a backstreet loan shark, started setting up offices across Dublin. Targets people with nothing, personally gives them cash. Personally rapes women who can't pay. Has a crowd who work for him who like to rip out the tongues of his clients' children. I'm not joking. Cops know all about him. Courts can't beat him. Long story. Half of Ireland will celebrate if something terrible happens to him. Not only is every debt written off, but the government can claim a good €40 million off his estate in Wicklow.

'And I know for a fact that every penny of that seized money, under a very special arrangement, will be given back to the people he stole it from.

'Danny Latigan is the first on the list, Aloysius, the first of four. Spuds, veg, beef.'

I'm smiling.

'Of course,' she says, 'you're on your own when you leave my side with that information. It goes without saying that while I have you in my loving Irish heart, if things go wrong I cannot have your back.'

And I'm smiling, filled with purpose as tiny, tingling raindrops lands on my hands and face, as more wind slides around my happy skin.

Nodding, I say, 'Goes without saying.'

'Good,' she says, 'so do you have any feedback other than that?'

'One thing,' I say.

'Yes?'

'No more hacking emails, no more listening to what I am not saying to you, no more American drones above me, okay?'

'Done.'

'You can end that right away?'

'Yes. Consider it done.'

'Then we have a deal.'

'Good,' she says. 'So shall we hard solve the Danny Latigan problem?'

'Yes,' I say.

Her phone rings. She looks at it, then to me.

She goes, 'Imelda Feather, yes.'

I watch her nod, and nod some more and I'm already feeling for the poor, misled guy on the other end.

'I see,' she says, and, again, 'I see. Well, that's a good one, I have to say. What an exciting moment it must be for you to ring and ask me that. I bet you're fresh from your editor's office having agreed with him what to say in this call, is that right? I bet you took a deep breath before you rang my number, did you? I imagine you tested your little digital recorder once, maybe twice, just to make sure it gets every word of this? Hmm? So here we go. Listen very carefully now. You do not have a picture because it didn't happen. And if I see one fecking word of this bollocks – one fecking word – I will personally knock you into the middle of next week and send you the bill. And it will be a bill from my lawyers that will make your stomach fall onto the floor via your fucking arsehole. I'm not even going to ask if you understand that. *Slán*.'

We walk back to her office, my arm around her to keep the chill from her mature bones.

She says she will set up a salary, will be in touch with the details, will get me what I need on Danny Latigan, but she realises I don't really need anything else at all.

I leave her at the top of the stairs.

I'm a few steps down when she says, 'Aloysius.'

I look back up, her hair like a tossed haystack. She's shaking her head, shaking it over and over as if in some kind of shock.

'Nice touch,' she says, lifts a finger and points at the picture opposite.

It used to be a beautiful image of an iron gate among trees on the left, of a road bending around to the right, of a mountain seemingly growing out of a field straight ahead.

But now it's of Ladies View, County Kerry, her favourite view in the world.

I shrug. 'Aye,' I say.

Chapter Sixteen

November 2016

A FALL down a long flight of stone stairs, a drunken tumble from a motorway bridge. A wheelbarrow of bricks from the top of a building site, a freak decapitation with a heavy spade. An overdose of heroin, a downed half-pint of mercury, a hand caught on the back of a moving trailer, a hanging from a lamp post, a blaze in a padlocked cabin, a rocky landing from a cliff fall, a mugging gone horribly wrong, an auto-erotic masturbation tragedy, a stumbled victim to a demented dog.

As I have been informed by my employer, my moral compass is all over the show. It's haywire, busted, buckled and fucked. But it spins and points at stuff the same as everyone else's compass does. It only tells me which way to go, which way is up when I need a direction, and, if my interpretation of that clashes with someone else's, then what's new?

Is your north the same north as the next person's north? Is your green the same, your black and white? Do you feel the same about charity, about war, disease, the electric chair, religion? Do you feel the same about matters of life and death as the next person?

At certain times, everywhere, certain life and death things are permissible, certain rules of engagement come into play. And hard times call for hard play, and hard play has hard rules.

At different times, for different causes, you will blame whoever made the man swing the bat. At certain times you will blame whoever swings it. At certain times you will blame the bat, the blunt instrument that does the damage. But before you decide where you join in and point the finger, take a look back at human history and be sure to point it everywhere, at every place you see on the map, at every tribe that ever walked it, right up until today, until right now, this minute. And then you can point it at me.

I know, you see, that with a certain world view these things I do are easy. And I know that, for me, this kind of work is strangely life-affirming, as if the power it bestows provides intention, accomplishment, resolution.

If you say to me, 'See this guy? His death will make many people happy because he's the biggest cunt in the country and, oh, here's some cash,' I'll say to you, 'That's interesting – what's his address?'

Like everyone else, I just want to get by in the way that suits me best and, in the end, to leave this world more peacefully and happily than I entered it.

In the big, grand scheme of things, at the age I am now, I reckon it doesn't really matter a damn whatever journey it is that brings me to that point.

★

'Evening Danny,' I say, and he turns as fast as he can in his heated swimming pool, eyes me through the mist lifting off the crystal blue surface of his own little mechanical lagoon.

He goes, 'Who the fuck are you?'

'Aloysius,' I say . . .

Chapter Seventeen

December 2016

CHRISTMAS 2016 and I meet with Martin and Imelda at a Dublin restaurant made loud by office parties and garish, sparkling outfits.

Our wee bash isn't so wild, but we are enjoying a fine meal and a few glasses of wine courtesy of the sozzled taxpayers all around us.

Martin has opened up a little, told me some of his story, how his daughter Kiera converted to Islam some years ago.

He's told me it was a bombshell among the old school Catholics of his family, how he feels they gave her Irish-based French-Algerian husband the cold shoulder, told Kiera her new fashion tastes didn't suit her.

It hasn't ended well in that, after a time, she grew tired of the insults and dirty looks, cut all ties with her family and moved with her husband to what they saw as an emerging caliphate in Syria. They felt, they said, it would be the best fit for them.

'Jesus,' I say. 'Hardcore.'

'Aye,' says Martin. 'She told me she was Muslim first, Muslim before Irish. Can't say that didn't hurt.'

I go, 'Right.'

He says, 'I went to France to meet the man's family and they were as shocked as we were. They'd no idea why. Just a couple of people who decided what was for them wasn't what the rest of us would see as healthy.'

And I'm thinking how stories like that are already known to me, how the world is full of stories like that, of people who find comfort in labels they were not born with.

Says Martin, 'We've come to terms with it in one way,' he says, 'me and my wife. We started out thinking she just needed a few wise words or a big bear hug, y'know? But we know now, from what we've heard from some of our American friends, that she's way beyond that. Way, way beyond that. And we've accepted it. Basically she's been swallowed up by this thing, this Islamic State world view, that fucking jihadi ideology, and she would by now expect the rest of us to want to give her a big hug, to want to tell her she's wrong. And, y'know, she would be ready to resist that, ready to fight it. The truth is hugging her would only reinforce what's already going through her head. There's no way back.'

I say, 'Have you lost her? Is that how it feels?'

He goes, 'It's like she's dead, Aloysius. It would be easier if she was dead, to be totally honest with you. We could start grieving, start to stop thinking about her, y'know?'

Her story, says Martin, has been in all the newspapers, all of them focusing on the fact that she's the daughter of a former senior civil servant.

'They want me to talk about it over and over again,' he says, 'but I have nothing left to say. I have lost my daughter and the whole thing has broken up my marriage, taken pretty much all I had. The press have suggested, in their own little way, that I don't say enough, that it's as if I'm not fighting for her, but they have no idea. All of this is about as personal as you can get, but they don't give a fuck. Imelda here has given me the best advice about how to deal with journalists you don't want to talk to, and she would know.'

I wait for it, but the pair of them just cut into their steaks instead.

'So, what's the best way to deal with journalists?'

And they both chew, look around them, enjoy the dark, happy, seasonal craic of this low-lit, bouncing wee restaurant.

'Ignore them,' says Martin, not even looking at me. 'Don't complain, don't explain. Don't feed them, they'll get greedy.'

And I'm wondering if he and Imelda have some wee trick going, some wee practical joke that fits the answer – if they ignored me on purpose.

'You're sure?' I say.

Imelda looks at me, says, 'What do you mean?'

'Well,' I say, 'there's truth in the idea that the best way to keep the focus on you is to ignore it.'

Imelda goes, 'Maybe with people, not with the press. People don't easily let go of what they are drawn to, but the press do. The press move on faster, have no emotional investment.'

Martin eats some more beef, wipes at his mouth. He's slimmer than I have seen him, must have lost a stone or more, but is eating like a horse tonight.

He says, 'Ignoring them is working for me. The lads reckon I shouldn't speak about it all, so I just say I can't talk about it when reporters call.'

'What lads?' I say.

'The intelligence guys,' he says.

'Who?' I ask.

'Our own lads,' he says. 'The Americans as well. They all say to say nothing. It's the Americans who get me updates on my daughter, but they don't want anything bleeding into the press, y'know?'

'What do you reckon to Irish intelligence?' I say. Neither of them have spoken about any official agency in this land to me.

Martin nods, says, 'G2? They don't know about our work and we're keeping it that way.'

I say, 'How do you know?'

'Because the Americans would tell me.'

Imelda isn't responding. She's drinking white wine to our red, looks well in the candlelight, looks somehow impressive when she eats, chews and swallows. I see how her neck is older than her face, but that it's classy, petite, pleasing in its symmetrical perfection. This may be the first neck I have ever really noticed, I reckon.

She sees me and I turn away, back to Martin, and her full blue, candlelit eyes linger on my cheek and now I just want to look back at them.

He says, 'The passing of Danny Latigan has brought a lot of joy to this town. Have you felt it, Aloysius?'

Imelda nods, takes a drink, 'It's been bloody good for the government too. Fifty million, he was worth, that fucker. Fifty million! They thought it was forty. Oh, and they kept the promise they made me.'

'I read about that,' I say. 'A wee Christmas bonus on the way for thousands of ripped-off people by the sound of it. Ireland does Santa. It's what you might call good PR, home and abroad.'

She laughs, 'That's right. It's all about the PR. I told you that back when we first met, didn't I?'

'You did.'

She takes a drink, 'It's been a while since we had a bit of the feel-good around here.'

'You're not joking,' says Martin.

They've put me up in an apartment near Shinay Associates, not that I'm encouraged to ever go to the office.

My role is to just be around, to stay fit, to stay out of trouble. I cannot, they say, be involved in any other work and I have, at least temporarily, removed the offer of my services from the Dark Net.

They advise very little drinking and no drugs. They advise keeping a low profile, they advise not making friends, not taking a lover. They advise reporting each and every suspicious thing I see or hear, keeping my eyes peeled for people watching, for who is coming and going into the places and spaces around me.

I don't know any of their contacts in government, any of their contacts anywhere. I don't know how deep they run, how high they go. I don't know if the taoiseach has signed off on this gig, or if it's all tight inside some black-ops department of the civil service or military. I don't know anything about when or how often they talk with people, and I don't really care. It's separation of state and state assassin, and that's the best way for everyone.

My glass is topped up again and I feel ready to drink some more. I'm tipsy, buzzing a little, feeling that lighter, happier, expectant, rolling mindset getting to work. I'm feeling I could drink a lot tonight, let my hair down a little, aim myself towards a nice, deep drunk and fall down laughing with my head spinning.

It's been a long time.

I've been training hard at my posh little gym beside a posh big hotel, and I've been losing weight and remoulding muscles. I've been taking advice on what to wear, shopping on Grafton Street, smelling better and cutting dashes. I've bought a suit and some nail clippers, slippers and a good watch, and life has never felt as easy to live.

And tonight I'm drinking in the safest, smartest company I could be in. I reckon my blank face is smiling two or three times a minute, some kind of rhythm, all caught up in some kind of cheery conversational beat that is playing out in my body language.

I like it when Imelda says, as we talk about what next year might bring for us, for Ireland, that feeling happy 'is a sign you're growing.'

'Yeats said it himself,' she says, and I see Martin roll his eyes, bracing himself for another quote.

She says,

'*Happiness is neither virtue nor pleasure nor this thing nor that, but simply growth. We are happy when we are growing*'.

Says Martin, 'Or when we're pissed.'

'Aye,' she says, 'that too.'

We call it a night at 11:15 PM. Imelda and I bid Martin a farewell in his taxi. We go the other direction, towards Ailesbury Road, where we will turn a corner, pass the office, stop at my apartment further along, and drop me off, and the cab will roll on to Imelda's house.

'Martin makes me sad,' she says, watching him go, his jacket seeming almost too large for him as he wanders towards an imminent sleep.

'How does he make you sad?' I ask. 'He's the chirpiest, smartest man I know.'

'He just does,' she says. 'He smiles through a lot of pain.'

And I think I can understand that a little.

Imelda taps the driver on the shoulder, tells him to pull over at the office. She pulls her laptop bag over her shoulder, asks me to go inside with her.

Keys and a code open the main door, a physically and mentally held security combination. She walks ahead of me on the back staircase, just the dark light of the winter sky clearing the route for us as we climb. I'm looking at her arse, her rounded maturity, her supple limbs pistoning as she climbs. And yet it feels like stealing, I feel guilty for nicking a boozy clock at my boss's bottom.

The picture at the top of the stairs comes into view. It's a moonlit night, the big wide full-fat yellow ball reflected in a peaceful pool, a pool shaped like a kidney, tiled by an artist. It's the late Danny Latigan's pool.

'Fuck's sake,' I say, and she turns to me.

'I know,' she says, looking over her shoulder, 'it's sick as fuck. You have to laugh.'

Keys and a code open the office door and, walking through in the dark, she plugs in another code at the door to her office. A little stamp-size disc slides out of the wall and lights up her face in a swimming-pool blue. She places her index finger onto it, the plate vanishes back into the wall and the door unlocks.

We're in, the room's blinds already closed against the night, and it's jet black when the door clicks shut. We stand there, momentarily, sensing the room, sensing each other, and I don't know what is happening.

I hear her walk and a desk light at the far end of the room flicks on, spotlighting her workspace.

'Coffee?'

'No thanks.'

'Me neither,' she says. 'There's something I want to show you.'

I sit on the plush, soft leather armchair in the dark, back

corner. This place intrigues me with its simplicity, with the crowded ordinariness hidden behind its smart security.

I have no idea who comes into this place, what gets said, what plots and calculations are made and how. I have no idea what kind of lists have been discussed and how, who, why and when. Who knows who gets the final say in matters of state discussed at the highest, quietest levels in a democratic republic?

All I know is the personal, the private, the what-works-for-me. I've learned the hard way that finding an ongoing thing to be, an ongoing thing to do, are among the best things a person can hope for in this world. For this world is not an easy place in which to do business over and over again, not a place in which to hunt for bargains, because the hidden costs can go sky-high.

Her back is to me and I hear the clunk of a thick bottleneck on a thick glass. I hear the glug. I hear it repeat.

She turns, walks, hands me a heavy tumbler, a harp engraved by an artist's hand on the side. There's a swinging whiskey in there that looks so clean you could drink it forever and feel better every day.

'*Sláinte*,' she says, taps her own against mine.

'*Sláinte*,' I say.

We drink and I look up at her, standing in front of me, her arm raised, her small, busy mouth catching the deep iron flavour of the long-aged drink.

'It's good fucking stuff,' she says, meaning it, turning, going back to her desk, grabbing the guest chair and dragging it over to the sofa.

She sits on it, close to me, right in front. She crosses her yoga-strafed legs, lets her shoes fall from her feet with a perfect kick of her heels.

I want to look at those tights, I want to see where they go, into the blackness that begins halfway up those darkened thighs. I want to get in among those point-blank shadows, to do the thing right in front of me, to fumble and search for sticky answers, for that devil's doorbell, for whatever hotspot of temptation I can find in there, and my instinct is saying to think very, very carefully about all of the above.

I interrupt myself, take a drink, enjoy the flavour, avert my eyes, stall the ball.

Yet I am thrilled at the idea of what type of underwear is on under there, and for a moment I picture some of those catapult pants, some pulled and tensed thong, and the image causes a fizzing in my groin.

'Pay attention,' she says, taking a drink, putting her glass down on the little coffee table to her left.

'Yes,' I say, and I prepare to clear my head.

She has a quality white envelope in her confident hands now, already been opened. She takes out a maroon document, a passport, and holds its face to mine.

I see the harp, that symbol which speaks of a musical, cultural, affable, extraordinary Ireland.

'One Irish passport,' she says, 'belonging to one Irishman.'

She reaches down, takes another drink, says, 'Funny that it takes a passport to make you real, isn't it?'

And I'm watching her, her neck pulling the whiskey down.

'Funny,' she says, 'that even a man like you needs one.'

I say, 'A man like me?'

'Yes,' she says, 'a man who is so very real, you know what I mean? A man whose presence can be felt in a crowd.'

And she doesn't look at me, takes another drink, says, 'So, you know what he's called, this man?'

I shake my head, and she's looking at me again.

She takes another drink, puts the glass down. Rubs one of her tired feet.

I watch her work the ball of her foot, then her toes, and I say, 'Go on. What's he called?'

Her eyes twinkle, her whole face twinkles, when she says, 'I want you to guess the name on the passport.'

'No idea.'

'Guess, for fuck's sake,' and she's laughing.

'A name I know?'

She shakes her head, 'Christ, you're slow as stop when you've had a drink.'

'Explain.'

'It's yours,' she said. 'It's your new passport, Aloysius, so you can travel.'

'Ah,' I say, and I realise I hadn't quite worked out what she was saying. And I think how that is a very interesting thing indeed.

'Right,' I say, 'that's interesting.'

'Good,' she says. 'Because your next mission, should you choose to accept it, is in the wonderful nation of Italy.'

'Ah, very good,' I say.

'Yes,' she says. 'It's like we're getting into the real spy stuff now, isn't it? Dodgy passport but issued by the government and all.'

'Aye,' I say, 'and you can call me Bond, Seamus Bond.'

She chuckles at that, heartily, and I swear it's as if she lifts her top leg a little, allowing enough room for an eye to get in for a quick theft.

'I'll remember that one,' she says.

And the top leg has settled on the lower one again. Now she is moving her shoulders around a little and all of this is combining to suggest pliability, to suggest suggestibility.

'So, Imelda,' I ask, 'what's my new name?'

She drinks and goes, 'No, no. You tell me. In fact, I'll give you three guesses.'

She rubs at that foot again, sore from the heels, from the long day and long night. That narrow, fine foot is so close I feel like reaching out and doing it a favour, but of all the things I have done against all of the rules, this one really does feel like a massive no-no.

But, what? What am I telling myself? I'm telling myself that there's no fear here, that it's only some kind of code that makes this invisible line. Only some code in my head somewhere, some unwritten rules about her age and mine, about her status and mine.

She's my boss, yes, but only because I consent. She's sixty-four, yes, but so fucking what? I'm forty. Whose issue is any of that and why is it in my head at this moment? What value have any of those numbers in here, right now, other than none?

The only issue here, the only one that makes real sense, is that there are some actions you cannot walk away from, actions that don't end when a heart stops and risk disappears. There are some things that stay around, that can mean all future interactions between two people get filtered through the memory of that one action forever. And . . .

'What's your first guess?' she says.

I go, 'Harry Duffy.'

She laughs, 'Nope,' waves the passport around, then presses it against her breasts.

I go, 'Johnny O'Shea.'

She laughs again, holds it tight, reaches down, rubs at that foot, which seems to be drifting closer all the time.

The laugh trickles away, and I watch as she kneads at the flesh on her sole now, massaging it with a steady hand, with experienced control.

It's a liberating thing about age, they say, that it makes you know what you want, that you have no time for putting up with the self-denial and internal bullshit anymore.

'Last guess,' she says, and her voice is serious now.

I go, and I'm just as serious, 'Ivor Hardon.'

Her eyes meet mine and we both laugh, both shake our heads, both as if saying 'No, no, no,' as if saying, 'Of course we're not thinking about that sort of thing.'

And we keep looking.

And we feel that tingling in and around ourselves now, the light air sparking between us, a switch turned on and a connection coming alive.

She clears her throat and I watch how her mouth and neck move. She brings the passport close, drops it onto my lap, reaches to get it. I let her hand go, watch as a tooth emerges to sensually bite at her own lip. I feel her opening me up, that cool, calm hand feeling inside and gripping me, removing my manhood, holding soft then hard around it. I look at her face, up to her forehead, to the lamplight on her mad, silver hair, and her eyes come up to me.

'So I see, Ivor,' she says, those blues flashing in the half dark. 'Looks just like the kind of fucking hard-on I could use.'

'It's all yours,' I say, long throbs of promise starting to push their way around my sex-starved body.

I reach out, a hand to the foot, slide it up the calf, up under the skirt. My eyes drop and I see her wrist moving now, her hand around me, its steady rhythm matching the cadence of my tick-tocking, explosive desire.

She has, I have realised, bent the passport around my cock. She is, I am certain, wanking me with a brand-new passport in my own name, a name I have not yet even heard, and she is so fucking insane that I want to love and kiss every stretched sinew of her over-perfect body.

'You're so fucking Machiavellian,' I say, my thoughts spilling from my mouth.

'I know,' she says, unsurprised.

'So fucking Machiavellian a guy would need a hard hat just to meet you.'

'At least,' she says.

I feel under the thigh, feel heat beaming, bearing down on my fingers from deep up inside.

As I turn my head I see the golden harp on her glass, a delicate lightness in this room of unknown corners and hard, unheard words.

And my gut starts telling me that this is some of the weirdest fucking sex shit that has ever happened to me.

She grips harder, pumps with full pressure now, looks me in my wet, blissed eyes as my free hand starts pulling at the top of her tights, starting to get this woman out of these clothes.

'I have to say,' she says, 'you feel like a fucking patriot tonight, Aloysius,' and moves over me with a hot, open mouth.

Chapter Eighteen

February 2017

NAKED IS strong.

It's not the skins you put on, it's the skins you shed.

The human hides – behind things, behind faces and clothes and words and cloaks, firing out notes to the world and hoping they come back and echo in his head just the way he wants them to.

The first thing we do when we get up or go out or move on is cover ourselves, get on some camouflage, break up the outline of what it is that we really are.

You're stronger without it in this world, without the hiding and bluffing. You're stronger in this world not by building on the weakness, but by ditching the weakness you have pulled in around you and over your head.

Shed skin, peel it away, layer by layer. Take your construction down, bar by bar, rivet by rivet. Strip it back.

Fuck the self-help stuff.

Fuck the life coaches.

Fuck that painting of yourself you're wasting your life with.

And whatever you're left with, whatever bits of dirt and grit that make you, make them ferociously yours and you will be fearless.

I found a man hidden behind a little boy. I found a man who can leave this world tomorrow without question, a man who can arrange the same for others without question.

Look at me and you will see no label, no badge, no ring, no symbol, no code, just some walking instinct, some unburdened, fluidly moving set of muscles that has come to know himself completely.

★

Liam Michael Marley is a paedophile with a track record as deep and dark as a fucking oil well.

He joined the priesthood because he knew another priest who felt the same as he did about those little singing-doll children in white, because he told him there was a place for him, a way to get among them.

If it hadn't been for the Irish priesthood of the '50, Marley's conscience might have got the better of him. He might have sought the help he needed and not helped himself. He might have sought the help of a noose or the help of a slap onto the ground from a tower block. But a safe paradise came calling, he answered it and – acting with great care, saying only the right thing to the right person – he found himself gaining friends

And when a group of people get together and feel the same way about one heavy thing, they're minded to feel the same way about another. And another. And another. And they will protect their own.

In time, Marley found himself in a club of hell where the rules are only that everyone must play the game and no one must know.

Marley had a way about him, a way of catching the eyes of well-meaning teachers, parents and those dumb-stuck fellow priests who prayed their way through their days. He went high in the church in Ireland, tearing open little bodies and minds as people bowed and smiled and asked him to bless their houses and cars, as they asked him to marry them, to see their loved ones off into the afterlife, to welcome their children into the world.

He went high, collecting big-name confessions, collecting big-name friends, and all the time he was as sick as all the secrets of Ireland put together in the head of one man.

And now, you see, he's writing the book. He's slipped his way through the system, served a silly twelve years for his crimes, and cleared off to travel Europe. He has looked up old friends and, from time to time, finds ways to continue his work.

Unrepentant Marley has found the space to write, to tell his obscene story, to explain what he and dozens of priests, what he and a long-dead politician and others got up to when the whiskey arrived and the children were summoned in the various and numerous homes in which he prayed and preyed.

He's got, you see, these dark, moment-by-moment details in his mind, and he takes great joy in writing them down. He tingles when he does it, when he types the names, the places, the ages, the acts, when he recounts the tears and screams. And he will write about how the stupid fucking state thanked him for blessing its flag as it let him reign and run riot how and where and why he liked.

Marley wants to publish the lot online. Everyone. Every date. He wants to name all of his victims, tell his readers where they are from. It's all just another massive act of betrayal to him and, as always, the power thrills him to the bitter marrow in his nasty old bones.

Marley is a few weeks away from uploading a tome to the Internet, which will be another body blow for Ireland. It is a confession too harrowing, too unacceptable, too completely at the end of its limit, and it is scheduled to appear at a time when a nation is trying to make a new future and shake away the untold horror of its past.

He is close to creating his very own bleak wind, to sending it rushing across the land, a wind that screams and burns as it moves down streets and over hills and right in through the front doors of people's homes.

Sooner or later, someone was going to end this man, to kill his life, stop his voice. Sooner or later, someone needed to hard solve this problem.

And that duty falls to me.

And I do not give one flying fuck that he is eighty years old.

★

It takes me four days to find him after a recent adventure he's had at a place in Slovenia where, with the right name and right sum, you can find parties for paederasts.

I track him in his old VW van as he tootles his way over the border and into Trieste, the north-west Italian region he frequently visits.

Marley, I'm told, has a few old dog-collared pals in the area and drops in by arrangement on occasion for, I assume, tea and note comparing. They go in groups to old churches, listen to Masses, have picnics in a countryside that causes a person marvel at the wonders of nature.

He's travelling slowly, and pulls off to the side of a quiet road between two peaceful little villages. He bumps his van over a kerb and between thirsty hedges, parking it up under some shedding trees.

I drive on, leave it half an hour, drive back, and it looks as if he's settling in for the night. A couple of miles from the sea, a couple of miles from the mountains, just from his surroundings he could be in Mayo or Clare. It looks like some place he might have passed through on his way to someone's home, where he grew excited about what lay ahead, where every beat of his approaching heart was more bad, bad, bad news for his imminent victim.

It's a place where a man might like to sit back and write for a while, to recall those moments in his life where he felt free, strong, important.

I park a little way along the road and wander back, weaving through the patchy hedgerow, under some trees and towards his yellow van.

The sliding door on its side is open, and he sits on its floor in his shorts, his bony, hairy, cream-white legs dangling out in the clean, cool air.

There's little hair left on top, but what is there is dyed black and fairly comical, as a little breeze flips and flaps it around one side of his head.

I watch as he turns my way, a big pair of shades on his thin, wrinkled face. He is still as he tries to work out who is walking towards him in the middle of nowhere.

It'll be a farmer, he'll be thinking. It'll be a landowner. It'll be some foreign fool asking for directions.

I get close and my eyes move to the van, to the outside details – the tyres, the top, the side window, the wing mirror.

I walk up now and push that wing mirror, a fleeting plan about how it might be used, but it gives, bends back too easily. It's not firmly in place, not strong enough for what I would need.

I bend, look along underneath, my eyes passing by his legs, from tyre to tyre and back again. I stand tall and look at where he is sitting, at the frame around the door.

'Hello? *Buongiorno?*'

There's a strip screwed along the bottom, a two-inch wide, thin aluminium piece on the edge, where he sits. It holds old lino to the floor at the base of where the door slides back into place. It'll have been added some time ago, picked up at a DIY store and locked into place to neaten things up.

'Can I help you?'

The van was made in the '70s, probably something of a collector's piece. It's a split-screen so-called T1 type model, not in bad order, all things considered. But it is bound to have had a couple of significant refurbs.

'*Señor!?*'

Probably a retirement present to himself, maybe something he picked up after prison, when he made it his plan to get on the road, to keep moving, to keep doing what he does.

I crouch down, scan all around me, a 360-degree turn, seeing if anything has changed, if there's anything I can see, anything or anyone that I might not want to see me.

I stand tall again, look at his collapsing old face.

He takes off his sunglasses, squints, goes, 'Do you speak English?'

No. This isn't a mugging gone wrong. This isn't a crash, a fall, a suicide, not even natural causes. This is a horrible accident.

He goes, '*Parlez-vouz Anglais?*'

I go, 'That's French, you prick. It won't get you very far in eastern Italy.'

And he's stunned by that, it jolts him back.

I move in closer, shove him to one side to see the details of this door frame, right where this aluminium strip starts and ends.

'What is this?' he goes.

I say, 'You got a screwdriver?'

We look at each other. He's got the look of a man who is thinking, but doesn't know what about. He's a man struck by confusion, bogged down and trying not to show it.

I look into his van, scanning for a screwdriver or something like it.

'Or something like it,' I say. 'A strong knife will do.'

He raises a thumb, jabs it in the direction of the tiny kitchen unit behind him. I look, can see a kettle steaming on the hob. There's a steel knife sitting on top of a plate. I push him to one side, reach across, grab it.

'What do you want?'

'Doing a minor redecoration of your van,' I say.

'You're Irish?'

'Yes.'

'Where from? North?'

'Fuck off.'

'What?'

'Fuck off.'

'No need for that language. I'm only asking.'

'Fuck off.'

I have the knife pushed under the strip. I lever upwards and it comes away easy enough. I bend the strip back and, brittle, the top of it breaks off leaving three inches of sharp silver shard jammed upwards. He looks down at it, this new, nasty point, this fierce new danger beside him.

I pocket the knife, slip off my shoes, push him to one side and climb in. There's a laptop charging from the leisure battery.

I say, 'What do you use with this? Disks? Flash drive?'

'What's that?'

'I said,' I say, 'do you use any disks or flash drives? How do you save your work?'

And he has stood, is walking away, slowly hobbling towards the road.

I rifle quickly around me. There are a thousand good places to hide something so small in here. I'm going to need his help.

I step out, shoes back on, and go after him, walking fast. I grab him by the arm and he tries to pull away.

'Hey,' I say, 'I'll make you answer me.'

He goes, 'Fuck you.'

I put him over my shoulder. He hits at my back, elbows me in the neck. His weight isn't troubling, but it's more than I expected. I drop him on the ground at the side door of the van and he's winded.

I grab the little finger of his right hand and bend it at its knuckles, folding it in three. I press the top of the nail hard, suddenly deep into the base of the finger, ramming intense pain through him, a red-hot, barbed spear.

He exhales hard, his jaw wide open, false teeth loosened. It's just air rushing out, just the stench of his stinking guts.

'Where do you store your writing?'

He points at his pocket with his other hand and I reach down, find a flash-drive shape in it, let him go.

'Oh Jesus,' he says, and falls onto his side, exhausted by pain.

I take it out of his pocket, look at it and put it in mine.

'Are there other copies?'

He looks up, rubbing his hand now, his eyes not open, not closed, not steady.

'Once more,' I say, 'are there other copies?'

'Of what?'

'Your book.'

'On the laptop and that thing you have. Nowhere else.'

'I'll ask you once more and then I'm going to repeat what I just did anyway. Any comment?'

He pulls back, pulls his hands back, tries to pull his old bones into the foetal position.

'What?'

I reach down, yank him upright, grab that little finger again and he goes, 'That's all, I swear.'

And I fold it over in three, put my thumb on the top of his nail and I push now as hard as I can.

His pain is again silent, yet almost visible in its emptiness, almost total. Only his back moves, sucking his spine in, his body slow-writhing, warping from the agony.

I reduce the pressure, let it go.

'Are there any other copies?' I say.

He shakes his head and I can't see tears but it's a face that deserves them. It's a face where they are noticeably absent. It's a face where tears are needed to finish the effect.

'I swear,' he says. 'I swear to God.'

I pocket the flash drive and lift Marley from the ground. I feel him relax, collapse in my arms as I step closer to the van. I lower him back to almost where he was, down onto the floor of the van so that his skinny, sickly legs will be hanging off the side.

His eyes refocus and fix on me when he feels the piercing tip of that aluminium spike on the back of his right thigh. He's going to say something when I force his descent, when I ram him down now onto the spike. His weight and the weight of my shove combine, and the cruel, sharp steel rips into the back of his thigh, right to the bone.

I stand back, look at him sitting there, one leg higher than the other, three inches pushing his right leg up, a thigh skewered like a chunk of chicken. He doesn't know whether to lean forward or back.

'Oh, Jesus Christ,' he says, frozen still. 'Oh Jesus Christ.'

He looks at me, his hands raising up and cupping below his face in some international sign of poverty, of innocence, some worldwide plea for any help of any kind at this minute.

He's giving it the 'why me?' treatment, and I know he knows why. I know a man like him always has the possibility of a terrible happening at the back of his mind, because even a man as buckled as Marley has, somewhere, somehow surviving amid all the misery, a simmering little pool of guilt.

I grab his right leg, work it back and forwards, needing to be as sure as I can that I rip through enough old muscle to tear open the femoral artery.

I feel bone grind against metal as I grip and shove, as I give it the 360-degree treatment and really get that wound opened. I see he is fainting, about to fall backwards as I work it, and I grab him by his throat.

'Stay with me, Marley,' I say. 'Stay with me, you bastard.'

I pull him up, see the blood on the spike, some on the floor, and I see it pissing out of the back of his leg like a busted wine box.

I drop him on the ground and he is trying his crawl into a ball thing, but gives up to stretch his neck, to make some kind of animal sound, something that would come from an abattoir.

'Move,' I say. 'Crawl forward.'

'Je . . . sus,' he goes, a shivering hand, grasping at a twig on the ground, his right leg quivering as blood bubbles and pumps out at high speed, rolling off his skin and soaking onto the soil and grass below.

'Move it,' I say, and kick his arse. 'Crawl forward you fucker. You've had a DIY disaster. Don't you want to get help?'

He tries, makes another gurgle sound, hasn't the strength to go further. He has maybe a minute now, if he's lucky, his blood spreading over the thirsty, blotting ground beneath him.

And he tries again to crawl, a pathetically weak grasp at a tuft of grass, and I reckon he's had enough.

I go to his face as he puts it on the ground, his eyes open. I go down on my hunkers, look at this old, dying man. I smile knowing this is no life wasting away, this is a waste wasting away.

'I fucking love my job,' I tell him, and he has no words for me. 'You know, it's times like this, I wish there really was a Hell.'

I say, 'It's good when something that must happen goes ahead and happens, don't you think?'

The blood slows now and I can see that little, blurred light of life he had in his face has faded away.

The final pumps and he is leaving fast, and I say, 'Goodbye, Father Marley.'

I watch as he breathes in once more, and I think maybe that's his last breath. I think this is another one biting the dust, another one who has bought the farm, another one popping the clogs.

That'll be the last stretch of this one's lungs, the last beat of this one's rotten, tired heart.

And this is one to remember, this evil old cunt. This is one for the memoirs, this view I have right in front of me right now.

I wave a hand, a friendly farewell to the imminently dead man from the guy who just killed him.

'Be sure,' I say, 'to tell God everything.'

And with his last, failing breath he says it, very slow: 'Aloysius.'

Chapter Nineteen

February 2017

I USE my time, my space, my car, and take a long drive north on long roads, sleeping on and off on the back seat, stopping at cafés and neon-lit fast-food flytraps as the need arises.

There's a viewpoint in Austria that catches my eye and breath, and I stop for a break, a stretch, a piss.

I climb over a wall, find a rock, bring it back to the car, and smash the old priest's computer and flash drive to smithereens. I scatter some of the pieces into the roadside bin, take the rest with me to ditch in another bin somewhere else along the way.

In half a week I'm used to Germany and closing in on the Netherlands, a place I've been missing a little, a nation with guts, class, brains, ambition and the strongest sense of fair play of them all, except they don't force that information upon you. For some reason, for a little moment, I just can't remember having had a bad day in Amsterdam, but I have to stop thinking about it right away before a few memories make themselves known.

I'm going to stop by with Tall Marianne, see how she's doing, tell her I never took her inherited car in the end, ask her if she's really found love.

Tall Marianne was always someone I could do business with, someone I could understand, who understood me. There are few questions you can ask Tall Marianne, few that she will answer anyway. And I never really asked her any at all. Likewise, there aren't many you can ask me, none that are worth your while asking, and Tall Marianne never asked.

She has no idea what I do, where I've been, where I'm going. She doesn't care. She lives in the now, a dreamy ultra-liberal moment where the past is barely prologue, where the definites of what just happened are just something that was, where the next second means everything and everything is fluid again.

I park up at 4 AM in the city, slip my seat back, pull the sleeping bag over myself, close my heavy eyes. I'm thinking how I'm thinking less these days, how my head isn't racing in and out of places I don't need it to be, it doesn't have me looking at strangers to add up numbers I don't need to add.

I'm exhausted but rested, hungry but feeling much more solid inside. I've found some kind of thing to do, some agreeable shape that fits some kind of grumbling hole.

I sail off to sleep, back in Amsterdam, just a day or so away from being back in Ireland, back to waiting, back to sitting around until I get number three on the list. And I see white lines flashing on long German roads in my mind's eye and it's all good.

★

Morning and I get three takeaway coffees, assuming Karson is still on the scene, and go to her door.

She opens, topless, plastic tits even bigger than they were, and beams. She throws her full arms around me and the coffees – one, two, three – smack the floor.

'You raggy Irish bastard,' she says, delighted. 'You really did disappear on me.'

'I really fucking did,' I say. 'I got a proper job.'

And yep, Karson is here, wearing only jeans, half awake, halfway through a bottle of Jack Daniels and very stoned.

'Ah bejesus,' he says in an accent he thinks is Irish, 'sure it's that Aloysius fella again.'

We shake hands and he goes, 'Oh man, I've heard some crazy stuff about you in the last few months.'

And I go, 'Don't believe a word she says.'

And he goes, 'I didn't hear it from her.'

Then that's him, turning away, going for his glass of bourbon, going for another smoke of that spliff in the ashtray.

He did that on purpose, dropped a quick bomb to get me thinking. I reckon that, for some reason, he likes to put me on my guard, to say unusual things. He looks out the window, tapping his feet to some music that no one can hear, and my instinct screams at me there's something that doesn't add up here.

Is this compact little guy just a really bad spy, still hanging around Amsterdam, tipping off his marks? Is he a shit spy who has fallen for this transsexual woman who is half a foot taller than him? Is he rebelling after being told by Langley to get his pants back on, stop drinking and smoking and get the fuck back home?

I just don't know, just don't know and just don't know. How do I move ahead on that? I just don't know.

We have omelettes in a dark, warm café off Vondelpark and, uninvited, Tall Marianne pours Tabasco all over hers and mine and Karson's and says she has missed me.

'I don't think I've been missed by anyone before,' I say.

'Aw, too, too sad, baby Aloysius,' she says. 'All your playing around in the shadows and shit, all that standing in the park at 5 AM and all that shit – Amsterdam is a tiny little bit less crazy with you gone.'

And all the time she is touching Karson's hands, eye contacting with him, kissing him as she chews her breakfast, crunches on her toast. He's too pissed to notice most of it, too pissed to stop smiling even when he is trying to get his grub into his face.

She's in the toilet and I tell Karson she's in love.

'I think so, yeah,' he says. 'A sweet, sweet girl, dude.'

'And you?' I say.

'Oh yeah,' he says. 'She's hard not to love.'

And I don't think he loves her, not as much as she loves him.

I say, 'Who told you about me?'

'What's that, buddy?'

'You said someone had told you stuff about me. What did you mean?'

He nods, chews on some egg, nods again, chugs some coffee. He goes, 'Yeah, yeah. How long are you around for?'

'A day. Maybe two. What did you mean?'

He nods again.

'I hear stuff,' he says. 'I know you think I'm CIA and all . . . ' and he takes another bite.

And I nod. 'Yeah,' I say. 'You more or less said as much. You're something like that. Maybe not their best man in the field, Karson, but you're a guy in the field in some way or another. A guy of use to them at the very least. Am I right?'

He puts his fork down, slurps some more coffee. He may not have cleaned his teeth in a few days.

'Yeah,' he goes, 'but I talk too much. It fits with the drinking and falling in love.' And he laughs at that. I laugh too.

He says, 'Some of the guys I work with at the university, some of them come and go, you know? I'm in communications, signals. The uni here is a bit of a hub, you know? We can pick up all sorts of stuff, push the envelope a bit with some of the tech smarts we have. Everyone is a little interested in us – Russians, Brits, Israelis,' and he laughs again.

I laugh, let him roll on.

'So much shit flying around Europe, Ireland at the one end and Russia at the other, and we can see a lot of it, man. If we want to, you know? What I'm telling you – and I shouldn't be telling you anything – is that we have some guys come and go, some of those guys you were referencing, you know?

'They like to use some of the equipment we use, like to piggy-back on some of the licences we have to get them into places that it's not so easy to get to otherwise, gain access to some of the material we can see, you know? We're basically academics profiling applications for high comms stuff, but if you wanted to see that stuff as potential assets for the US, as ears and eyes, then you could call it that. Explains a lot of the funding that comes our way, you know, from the State Department, you know? Basically, what I'm telling you Aloysius, is that some of our visitors don't always travel under their own names.'

Tall Marianne is back, fast finishing her breakfast. She always tells people she has a great appetite for pretty much anything that can be put into one's mouth.

'Cutting-edge work by the sounds of it, Karson,' I say. 'And how does this link back to me?'

Karson slurps some more. He looks at Tall Marianne, looks at me. He shrugs.

'You got some ears on you,' he says. 'Eyes and ears. On you in Dublin, on what's going on over there, on what you're doing over there, what you're doing in other places.'

I shake my head, acting confused. I know some of this, I know Imelda and Martin asked for me to be tracked. I also know Imelda called it off after I came on board, but I'm not making any confessions to this guy.

I say, 'What do you mean?'

He shakes his head, laughs.

'Aloysius,' he goes, 'listen buddy, us two didn't think we'd ever see you again. I haven't come looking for you and I've never tried to get in touch with you, okay?'

'Yeah, why would you?'

'Well,' he says, 'T Marianne wanted to see if I could find you, asked me a favour, wanted to know if you had died or some shit, after she found out that car she gave you never moved. I did a little search, checked out a couple of records. We have good equipment man, I'm telling you. So, yeah, there you were. On records, in Dublin. And these records, you know, they had been opened and compiled by some of the guys we've been talking about, you know? And they had a lot of detail and shit, you know? Like they really had been tracking your ass.'

'Okay,' I go. 'Well, I've travelled a lot, done some stuff I shouldn't have. I'll be one of thousands of people they're keeping an eye on. No biggie.'

Karson nods. 'Yep,' he goes, and eats his last bit of toast. 'You could think of it that way.'

And he looks at me, nods again.

And I say, 'But?'

He goes, 'Listen Aloysius. I'm not talking bullshit. I'm not too interested in bullshit. I just want you to know I'm doing you a favour. I'm doing you a favour because this woman here – who loves the fucking hell out of you – told me thirty minutes ago that she wants me to tell you this stuff. So I'm just telling you. You do what you want with it.'

I look at her and she's embarrassed, blushing, munching bacon.

'I've heard all this,' she says. 'I didn't know what to do but it was better that you heard it than you didn't hear it, right?'

I go, 'Right. Thanks.'

He goes, 'In the end, it's probably pretty meaningless to you, but there are eyes and ears, okay.'

I go, 'Okay.'

'These guys,' he says, 'they know you're working off a list, okay?'

And my stomach does some kind of tiny roll.

I go, 'Okay,' try to give nothing away.

He goes, 'And here's the rub.'

Oh shit.

I go, 'What?'

'The list has four names. Two names are scored off. The last name? The word is you're not going to like it.'

The details this guy knows are incredible, worryingly bang up-to-date. I have no idea if he's pulling some move on me, but he knows stuff he should not know, stuff even I do not yet know. At least I know that on one impressive, dangerous level, he is not bullshitting.

I go to speak, feeling dazed, totally vulnerable, and all I say is, 'You couldn't know . . . '

'Ya think? Ya fucking think, man? Hey buddy, the guys I know, they look at the world from the inside out, from the screens outward, from the phones outward. They don't have to get inside anything anymore, they are fucking inside before you come along and press buttons and make calls and look shit up. You can assume they are above your head in drones and satellites 24/7. There is information fucking overload going on. There is more intel out there on people than they know what to do with.

'The shit I'm telling you is so fucking minor, so fucking unimportant, that it isn't even held in a secure file. It's in a file called "Ireland", and it's got a fucking laughing leprechaun as an icon, you get me?'

'Right.'

He goes, 'You go on the dark net and you think you're hidden? Man, you go on the dark net and you're more interesting, that's the truth. There is no hidden. There's just degrees of how interesting you are. You and your "hard solving", yes? You and your five stars for doing what you do all over Europe, yes? Guys I know are sitting around watching stories like yours like it's a fucking soap opera, taking bets on who you will be sent to get next. You think you operate in secret? You're fucking crazy, man. I heard you just made an old man bleed to death. I heard you spent a day beside someone's pool and watched them drown. I heard you pulled some guy into a damn dog pit and stood there as he got eaten up. You don't have any secrets, man. Now isn't that supremely refreshing?'

I go, 'Yeah.'

Tall Marianne starts humming to herself.

And I don't answer, just drink the last of my coffee.

He goes, 'You want me to tell you the name on that new passport?'

And I say, 'Yes.'

He goes, 'Marcus Tempo.'

I go, 'Right.'

He goes, 'You going to drink whiskey and fuck your boss again?'

I go, 'Right.'

He goes, 'Right.'

I say, 'So finish the conversation.'

'What?'

'Tell me the rest.'

'What rest?'

'The last name on the list.'

'I don't know, man, that's the truth. It's written somewhere, not on anything that can connect to the Internet. But the guys picked up chatter, some stuff about it being a hard decision at the end, that it's a betrayal and that they can't tell you until the time is right. Said you're not going to like it, said you'll have to be bluffed into it. I guess these people – this agency you work with – it wants to close all this shit off, Aloysius. This damn list is final, then it's over, you know? Whatever that means to you, is whatever it means. Be careful who you trust.'

And he goes to drink up and there's no coffee left.

He says, 'I guess if you're the guy doing the what you call "hard solving", you can at least be sure that number four isn't you. Or at least that there's no sign of you on any list, not yet anyways. I'd stay wide awake to that possibility, though. Be careful who you trust, my friend.'

I smile at Karson.

'Cheers,' I say.

He goes, 'If you get the last name, call me. I'll tell you the direction of all this shit. Or don't call me. I don't give a fuck.'

I say, 'Cheers.'

'Hey no problem,' he says. 'Let's go get drunk and baked and not talk about it any more.'

★

I sit at the *Sunflowers*, try to find a simple, uncluttered place in my head. Everything that had been blossoming feels now like it's closing, everything that had fitted is now gripping too tight.

I've gone from being all fully charged to flat. I've been hit by a smart missile, a know-nothing boy from the sticks, hit around the head by a professor. My ducking and diving has just been a dance for some to watch, a stupid little set of moves watched by judges who couldn't help themselves but laugh.

Frankly, it's fucking embarrassing.

I need to see Imelda, to ease some truths in and out of her. Yet the one thing I cannot do, until I am face-to-face with her, in a neutral space, a thousand miles from fucking anywhere, is talk to her about this stuff.

I go and look at a self-portrait and mull over all the people that Van Gogh sees every day. I think how the greatest trick in the world would be to have the world walking before him, with not one of them ever knowing he was looking back, noting what they're looking for, the shape of their faces, the glisten of their eyes and pondering how to paint them as they stare innocently at his concentrating face.

I find myself reaching for my ear, ludicrously working out a way to slice it off just like the Van Gogh story says. I'm here now and thinking how I could cut it off in this museum and bleed all over the place. I'd be on the front of every newspaper in the land, being read about on screens across the world, and it would give me more control over who sees me than living in some shadow world ever does.

And it's all the opposite of what I want. The exact opposite. I want nothing out there on me, no notoriety. I wanted to find a warm cave in which to be, an easy place for my mind, body and soul. I asked Imelda for that and she promised she could deliver it. And now what? I am a sitting, quacking duck.

This entire operation, this ridiculous dirty, dreamy Irish PR scam, is a farce.

I should not have had that joint.

I need to lie fucking down.

I need to go and find a bed and lie fucking down.

I need to lie down, sleep, wake up and, as best I can, be still and silent.

I need to watch the watchers, those people who pass by to take a look. I need to see what they are thinking, what shapes their faces are making when they look at me. I need to know who's who and what's what and why.

I can no longer be in the dark.

I am insulting my own intelligence by being in the dark.

I need to watch the watchers.

And how the hell do I do that?

I don't know.

I no longer know.

You know what? I'm no longer smart. I'm now stupid. And I'm smart enough to know that I'm stupid.

You know what?

No, here's the craic, here's the point I'm trying to reach in my own head here.

Fuck this for a life.

Chapter Twenty

February 2017

I'M IN an Internet café at the Hook of Holland, and put in a Facetime call to Imelda. She has always told me to speak my mind with her yet now there's so little I can say.

She beams out of the screen, tells me she's glad to see me looking so well, wonders how I feel about my trip to Italy?

'Peachy,' I say, and she fires me a sideways glance.

'Nice,' she says, a little suspicious. And then, right away, 'I want you to head to Belfast, Aloysius. Ring me when you get there, okay?'

'Why?'

'Number three on the list,' she says. 'That workable?'

I say, 'Yeah, grand.'

Whatever. Fuck it. I might as well go to Belfast and do number three while standing in the middle of the road. I might as well do number three in a live television studio.

Going to Belfast is like going anywhere in this world now, I have no anonymity, no privacy, no space of my own. And, I'm thinking, if the Americans already know absolutely everything, then surely the British at least know a large amount of it. And if the British know it then, one way or another, MI5's massive operation in Belfast knows it. They probably already know about this call.

I reckon I might do number three on stage in front of an invited audience of security officials. I might do number three in a police station while shouting out my name. I might do number three all over the fucking Web while confessing at high volume to numbers one and number two.

I book the car on the ferry to Harwich and, onward, on the Liverpool-Belfast.

It's raining now, a cold and wet spring, and I've hardly slept on the rowdy, boozy weekend vessel to the Northern Ireland capital.

There's a cursory glance from a customs official as I drive off the boat and into the city, a half wave of a wet hand as the wipers half reveal who I am.

'Whatever,' I say, driving off. 'I'm a mass murderer, so I am.'

Booked into a cheap hotel, I feel the gloom like fog around me, a cloud reminding there is now a complete pointlessness to all of this cloak-and-dagger bullshit.

I see the corner of a bible in a drawer and I hoak it out, wish there really was some book with all the answers. I flick open its pages for no reason and see two thick, black pubic hairs pressed between the pages of Exodus.

I go, 'Fuck's sake.'

I take myself to a dive bar for some mood symmetry and, standing at the doorway, make the call to Imelda, a pint of thick, cold Guinness in my hand. I believe she may be a woman who wants me to kill someone I don't want to kill, and I don't understand. This is, right now, a woman who may very well want me dead very soon, and that makes clear sense. This is the sort of shit I expected at the outset. This is the stuff my instincts warned me about.

'There's a wonderful up-and-coming politician in Belfast called Martha McStay,' she says, before I say anything.

I go, 'Right. And what's your opinion on caution, on security?'

'I'm all for it. What's yours?'

'Don't you think you're maybe a little loose with it sometimes, given what we know about the prowess of our bigger brothers in the world?'

'Aloysius,' she says, 'don't make the mistake of overemphasising the importance of what we are doing to the rest of the world. This is about us, the Irish. Everyone else has their own troubles, okay?'

I say, 'You're not as forward thinking as I used to think.'

'You'd be surprised,' she says.

'That's what people say when they have no useful answer.'

There's a silence.

She goes, 'Maybe you should take a break, come in for a while. Maybe this is proving too much for you.'

And I can't say any more to her. I can't tell her what I know about Karson, that I know she has just plotted another murder in someone's ears, that the word 'betrayal' has been shooting around in my head like a rock on fire. I can't tell her that I know what is going on here, and that at the same time I haven't a fucking clue. The more the picture clears, the more it moves away from me.

She says, 'I cannot have any shivering and pissing yourself and crying out there. Get away to fuck with your weakness. It's time for a talk.'

'You misunderstand,' I say, 'completely.'

She snaps it back, 'I don't. I assess and draw conclusions, and I'm fucking good at it. Don't try and trump me, young man, you haven't got the brains.'

She pauses again.

I go, 'I have no issue with this job and I don't give a shit who this next person is. I just don't think you're considering all the options or looking around all the corners. Not when it comes to your communications. Let's leave it at that.'

'You're boring me, Aloysius,' she says. 'You're boring me during what is an extremely important set of moments for our nation, during an extremely delicate conversation we are having which impacts directly on the future of our country. I need a strong, bold and complete performance from you in the very near future while you are in Belfast. I need potatoes, vegetables and I need fucking meat. Is that going to happen?'

I say, 'Yes,' and I sink a third of my pint.

She goes, 'Good. Right. See that it does. We will talk in Dublin.'

I go, 'Right.'

She says, 'I have to say, Aloysius, this is the first time I've felt disappointed by you. You always give me more than I expect to get, which is a charming way to behave. But this is the first time any of your communications with me have not met that standard. It's the first time they have been, what shall I say, below par.'

I go, 'Maybe you've been spoiled. And, anyway, below par is a good thing. Look it up.'

The silence crackles with her rage, or maybe it's some American guys laughing at our chat.

She goes, 'Do not get smart with me.'

I say nothing. I cannot say what I need to say, cannot steer this conversation. I kind of want to laugh, or sniff or shout or speak in tongues, give her something completely off-centre, some kind of code, that gets her thinking, not judging.

But I can't. I just have to let her say her bit.

She goes, 'I'll see you in the fair city.'

And I'm pressing the button when I hear her say, 'And good luck.'

Whatever.

And whatever luck is coming, bad or good, it won't have a problem finding me because everyone knows I'm standing here big and plain as day.

★

Eight days later, we've hit March 2017, and I have all I need to know. Matha McStay, an elected MLA in Northern Ireland's parliament, is twenty-nine. She has a community-worker boyfriend and was pregnant last year but miscarried. She lives alone on the seventh floor of a ten-storey tower block on a working class, north Belfast estate. She runs marathons, likes to box and has many enemies, many friends. She was once handed a three-month suspended sentence for attacking a man who got too fresh with her.

There are two mean-looking guys who drive her around, take her to Stormont, to meetings, to events, to her lover's place. They wait for her, take her back, take her wherever she needs to go, and they look like they will kill anyone who threatens to bring her any harm.

They're not police, these guys. They're not official, but more likely supporters, two heavies attached to her because they are attached to her hard political views, to listening to the specific sounds she is making in a place where politics is mostly noise.

I've watched Martha McStay in a number of situations, often smiling, often sparking smiles on the faces of those who meet and greet her. Her body language, and the language of those around her, tells me that no one, male, female, rich or poor, ignores Martha McStay. I've watched people fawning, I've watched people come close to bowing in front of her.

Whatever she has done in her past, it is completely overshadowed by her presence in the here and now.

She impresses, she sexes-up every environment she enters, and I find it hard to take my eyes off her.

On Monday, two days ago, Martha McStay spent an hour with a psychiatrist who has a reputation for working with people suffering from the hardest effects of post-traumatic stress disorder.

On Tuesday, Martha had her goons take her to a chemist's where, with a prescription, she loaded up with strong anti-depression medications before she disappeared into her flat alone, and sat up late into last night.

During the evening, she pulled her coat collar up and a hat down before walking twenty minutes to the back of a pub. And there a member of staff privately passed her two bottles of vodka, which she put into a little rucksack, and carried home.

Today is Wednesday, the day when, without fail, Martha McStay takes a yoga class in a community centre on the estate where she lives.

I watch now as she leaves it, laughing and chatting and smiling with a friend at the door, bidding farewell as she walks across the car park, past two shops and into her own building. She is not escorted for this class so close to her home, her two heavies – as with last week – nowhere to be seen.

From behind, as she stands at the lift doors, checking her mobile, I see a short, petite, crafted body in Lycra. There isn't an ounce too much flesh, not an ounce too little. Her bottoms are black, the runner's boob tube pink, the towel slung over her shoulder, white. Her arse cheeks are smooth as boiled eggs, as hard as apples, would get a second look from a man with no head. I cannot resist informing myself loudly and clearly that there is very little, if any, underwear going on there.

I'm moving as the lift doors open. She finishes on her phone, looks up, sees an older woman exiting.

'Hiya Fiona,' she says. 'How's life?'

'Not too bad, love. Keeping well.'

'That's good.'

Martha and I get inside and she looks at me, smiles, almost makes me smile back.

'Where are you going?' she says, hitting button seven, her face all sweet and quizzical, a little Audrey Hepburn meets a little Demi Moore, a flaming firecracker who must have been asked out a million times.

'Ten please.'

The doors close and I can smell piss and bleach and a thousand Saturday nights and I feel like mentioning it, but what's the point in doing anything like that with someone who is about to die.

And up we go.

She stretches her neck a little as we approach seven. The lift stops, the door clicks, is about to open.

I step in front as she's about to move.

'You're going to ten,' I say.

And she smiles, 'Nope, you're going to ten. I live on seven.'

And I'm stern now, 'You're going to ten.'

I stand with my back to the door and she doesn't blink, looks into my eyes the whole time, getting some kind of measure of me. And I know she is not scared.

The doors close, the lift moves.

She says, 'Who precisely are you?'

'Tell you in a minute.'

The door opens and a man, maybe fifties, is there.

'Well Martha,' he says.

I gently touch her elbow, lead her from the lift.

'Well Stevie,' she says. 'Did you get your toilet fixed?'

'I did,' he says, raising a friendly hand, a little wave for someone he likes. 'Thanks for your help.'

'Not a bother,' she says.

And the door closes on Stevie.

She walks easily and I lead her to the service door behind the lift. I've already broken it open, and I walk her through. She is completely calm, totally compliant. It closes behind and we climb fifteen steps, open the pre-broken door onto the roof. We both stand for a second, feeling the wind, looking around at the city skyline sloping down and running across the enormous valley and into the lough before us.

'Start talking,' she says. 'I think it's time, don't you?'

I take her elbow, walk to the edge, a half-filled square car park below. We are on the tallest, ugliest building around. I'm calculating that we have a minute, maybe two, before someone notices people up here.

'End of the road, Martha,' I say.

'Off the roof?' she says, more surprised at the method than the murder.

There's small, yellow steel fencing – a basic, box-ticking safety measure, two-feet before the drop. I go to step over it. For the first time, I feel her resist.

'Two witnesses saw you with me,' she says. 'Have you thought about that?'

'Saw what?'

'You.'

'What will they say?'

I gently urge her onward, a little pressure on her elbow.

'They'll describe you. You know they will.'

'Saying?'

'Tall, dark, handsome.'

'Thanks. The woman at the bottom didn't look at me. The man at the top looked at my shoes, at the side of my face and then your arse.'

'Side of your face is enough,' she says, the wind blowing her bobbed hair now. 'You have a memorable profile.'

'You have a memorable arse. If I was asked to describe it, it would soon start to sound a lot like other memorable arses.'

'You're funny,' she says.

I urge her a little again and she gives. Steps over the fence, still a shade resistant, but still not scared. I move her in front of me and consider I've never had a situation like this before.

'What is this?' she says. 'Revenge? Did I do something to you?'

I don't answer.

She goes, 'They always do say revenge is a dish.'

And I'm losing track of how and what to think about this woman.

'You're not what happened to you, you know,' she says to me. 'You're what you choose to become.'

And I'm trying to focus here, batting her words away inside my head, clearing the mind to let the training kick in, the clinical coldness, the mindset which likes to negate all the scales and balances of the day.

'Who are you?' she says, and I'm turning her back to me, facing her towards the edge, and she doesn't make it difficult.

She says it again, speaking up now, her words diluted by the rushing air. 'Seriously. Who are you working for?'

I'm not talking, not lying or telling the truth. And still she is here, still fighting for my attention, fighting and winning.

'You can tell me a half-truth,' she says, 'or even just a quarter.'

'I'm in PR,' I say.

'Wow, a changing industry.' She almost shouts it.

'Evidently.'

The wind is firm against our faces now as I push her gently ahead, right to the end of the cement, to that ninety-degree shelf, to the death line.

I'm ready to shove her in the back now. I will see the wind swoop around her hair as she goes, I will see something in front of me become nothing. I will hear the punch of flesh on cement and already be five steps from here.

But she turns fast – agile, confident, with zero distance to spare. She faces me, eyes on my neck, bold as a bullet, and it takes me by surprise. She looks up, grins, alight and alive.

And I'm time-wasting here, wasting time I should use, making the seconds soft when they should be hard. I'm killing time at killing time. And I really like looking in her dark, dark eyes. I feel her hand take mine, feel it lifting up to her chest. She opens it, places it on her heart and I feel her rhythm, slow and strong. Now she puts one hand on my chest, feels the beat, slow and deep.

'We're alike, us two,' she says, and she's looping my fingers around that tough pink Lycra boob tube.

'We go to the edge and sometimes we fall,' she says, 'but falling is beautiful, failure is beautiful.'

And I feel my hand tighten around her top, backs of my fingers onto her warm, silk skin on this cold roof, as she says, 'Take a good grip.'

And Martha McStay lifts her arms, spreads them like wings, and falls back, closing her eyes, a beaming smile, feet on the ledge, leaning into the sky, an act of faith without faith, of trust where there is no trust.

I have to catch my breath, harden my grip, to stop her from falling.

The Lycra stretches, the wind rushing up between her breasts and I see now they're not there. As she lies back further her top stretches and thins and I see fakes built in to the clothing, two upside-down smiles on her chest, two eyebrow scars where breasts once were. And she's on her tiptoes, her only contact with the tower block. My arm is fully stretched, her top is as pulled as it can be. And now I have to lean back or she will surely plunge.

I reckon the wind could just whisk her away at any second, a firm gust would just lift her, float her out into the sky like a light little pixie, her hair dancing around her face.

I look at my hand, at how one movement will hard solve problems for people, will complete what I have been sent here to do, and my hand is firm and strong and holding fast.

'What's your name?' she calls, her voice louder, yet just audible, just touching my ears before it gets shooed away by the wind.

'What is it?' she calls it again, head tilted back now, hair scattering about her face.

'Aloysius,' I say. 'It's Aloysius.'

And this mad, wounded woman has me smiling, holding her life in this killing hand and grinning along with her.

She goes, 'Aloysius – I *love* that name. It's fucking *poetry*.'

And, good and loud, I go, 'Right.'

And she says, 'You can let me go now.'

Chapter
Twenty-one

Russian Military Training Base
Tajikistan, Central Asia

April 2008
Evaluation Interview #21 – Final Session

'I'LL BE driven to Israel, enter the country with a fake ID as a Russian Jew. There won't be a problem with the language, with any questions about my past.

'When I get there I go dark, disappear in Tel Aviv for a couple of months. They say they have a cash-in-hand job for me, working on the beach.

'And when I get the call, I go ahead, collect the weapons from some location, make my way to Gaza and complete.

'And after I'm finished? I don't know if I'll be alive or dead. If alive, well, the only order is never to speak of it, to disappear into Western Europe and never look back.

'Then, yes, maybe go back to working in France, maybe over to London for a while. Maybe even back to Ireland or America, who knows? If I need work, I can put my hand to most stuff. If I need to put some bigger money together, I can maybe get involved in a bit of mercenary work, maybe even get some work somewhere as a hitman, an assassin-for-hire. I hear there's always money to be made in that area. I've been wondering, to be honest, if there is a market in accidents.

'Nothing troubles me just now, that's why all of this is working out for me. Not the future, not even the past. Even if I died during this thing, it wouldn't trouble me. If I live, well, I've been running since I was seventeen. Running some more won't trouble me.

'You know, they always knew it was me who beat that priest to death on his floor, but they never wanted to pin it on me. It was too messy, raised too many questions, would have opened the door on all of what we now know, and no one in power wanted to open that door. They just said it was a break-in, that some lunatic had smashed the window in and smashed Father Barry's head in during a mission to steal some gold, but they knew it was me.

'I stayed at that place for another six years, untouched, untroubled, before deciding to get the fuck out of Ireland on my own terms. I reckoned I had guts, dirty guts but guts, and that I could make a life somewhere.

'So, despite all of the past, I'm on no register, no wanted list. To Ireland, I'm no one, someone long gone, maybe someone who was never there.

'No loyalties, that's me.

'No one loyal to him, that's me.

'That's why you guys went for me, isn't it? You read something in me, something you could use. You saw someone who had no love of anything, someone who presented no risk of getting torn away.

'So let's just do what we have to do in Israel and it will be as if we never met, as if you never heard of some guy from a milk crate called Aloysius.

'If I die, sure you can just sing a sad song about some Irish guy and that'll be fine, too.'

Chapter Twenty-two

March 2017

SUNDAY IN Dublin.

I've dropped the car off at the docks, am walking back through the squeezed city. There's a light, barely wet Irish rain on my face.

That car, I'm thinking, goes back into some steel box for safe keeping or, more likely, gets shipped across the sea. It gets cleaned and re-sprayed somewhere, gets remarked and rolled out for someone else, someone else unofficial with official connections.

How many of those sorts of cars are there in this world? How many things or people or places get this official invisibility, this sanctioned cloak around them?

Fuck only knows. No one would ever tell me these things. You get a role and you play it. You do all this rule breaking within the rules, that's how the game works.

Me? I'm just a guy who was given a car, a guy given some stick-on number plates, a guy told to replace them two or three times as I did my travelling. Who by? I don't know. Whoever left the car on my street and put the keys through my letter box. Maybe the same person that takes the car away again, now that I've left it down at the docks.

A priest told me one time I would one day be the sort of guy who calls at someone's door, cold and hungry, and asks for something to eat. He looked at me and said that was what the future held for me.

But he said in my case it wouldn't just be a case of being hungry, it would be a case of being hopeless. He said I was bad luck, that I would always have it because I made it, I was a source of it. He said that was what went on in my heart – bad luck.

He said I would call at the door of the house and the guy there would know me, would be asking me what the problem is. And I'd be telling him the problem is I'm hungry, and he'd be all, 'Why are you being so strange? Of course I can get you some food, but what's wrong? I don't understand. What happened?'

This priest told me it wouldn't take long before I'm shouting it, shouting out that I am all empty inside and need to eat something. And the priest told me the guy at the house would kick me out, call me an arsehole as he shoved me out the door, his wife looking on from another room, head shaking.

The priest told me, 'That can go on forever, Aloysius. You can go calling at every door in the street and everyone will be trying to understand what happened, how it came to this, and they will never get it.

'It can go on forever, people not being able to comprehend. They'll say you used to be fine, but now you're at the door begging for an apple, a bit of bread or toast or a lump of cheese.

'They'll say "How can this be? What are we misreading here? Why is he being so forceful about this?"

'People won't understand that you speak the simple truth. And you will get shunned and shunned again because people feel that they suddenly don't know you and your new ways, but it's just the old you, the old you, but hungry and tired and fed up with the world.'

The priest said this would happen to me because I didn't fit, that sooner or later I would always have a hunger and always be misunderstood.

'You're like me in that way,' he said. 'We're both misunderstood. Your problem is bad luck, you have it in you, it's where you're going, it's what you will be to people and they will come to realise it. You'll ruin people's hopes and hearts, so you will. You will be a man nobody wants, showing up at their homes all sincere like a cancer. That's where you're going. All little bastards like you end up like that.'

He said, 'My problem, Aloysius, is that I'm drawn to people like you, drawn to help, to do what I can. It's my mission, the path God has asked me to take, and I must take it.

'But it means that I collect all the bad luck, it means so much of it rubs off on me, that I too end up ruining lives and hopes and dreams.

'We're the same, you see. We're one and the same, you and me.'

He was saying I was already lost, lost and gone before I was found. He was saying he was the only one I could and should trust.

And I've dropped off my invisible car at an unknown location after a trip around Europe on which I didn't actually go. I've knocked at doors, and what kind of a man was I, standing there, when the person opened them?

The priest was wrong. I am worse than a hungry man. I am worse than bad luck. I am much, much worse than a guy who might seem a little strange at your door. I'm a fucking nightmare,

I'm adversity like you never knew before. I'm the last day, your last contact with the world. I'm the fucking Grim Reaper. I'm not bad luck, not some random event that goes wrong, I'm a fucking planned and executed dose of the fucking end, I'm your statistic, your number, and when I am up at your door you better not even answer.

★

Martin Gird sits on the steps leading up to the front door of my really very good-looking apartment block.

'Did you hear about the three holes in the ground?' he says.

'No. Tell me.'

'*Well, well, well,*' he says.

'Well now,' I say, 'my joke detector tells me there might be one around here somewhere.'

'Haha, not here my friend. But I do think this specific situation needed a—'

'Well, well, well.'

I drop my bag, take a seat beside him, look across the quiet, Anglo-Irish grandness of the posh outh Dublin street.

'Enjoy your travels?'

'I note you didn't use the word holiday.'

'You note correctly.'

'Aye,' I say. 'It's a fucking weird line of work though.'

'You're not wrong,' he says, passes me a newspaper.

I look at the image of a line of priests on their knees, praying for the rotten soul of Father Liam Marley.

'We have them on their knees,' he says. 'They have to pray for the old fucker's soul and at the same time pray for forgiveness from the rest of the country. They've a lot of praying to do.'

'Yep,' I say. 'And nothing fails like prayer.'

He goes, 'Do you see what it means though? It means there's another pile being driven into the cesspit we called decent society around here. Another fucking leg up for the new day, y'know? You see it means we're moving on another little bit, thanks to you? You see that, don't you Aloysius?'

And I go, 'Aye. I see it.'

Martin smiles at me, a smile that makes the outer edges of his eyes curl, one that tells me there is no distance between that smile and the mood of his mind.

'Good man,' he says, clearly happy yet clearly tired from co-carrying the secret weight of all of this brutal engineering. 'You'd better go in.'

'Meaning?'

'Meaning she's waiting for you. I think you've pissed her off, to be honest.'

'Nah,' I say. 'Sure she knows I'd kill for her.'

I leave Martin on the step, stretching his back. I go through the front door and turn right to get into my own pad. I didn't even know she had a key, but then of course she has a key.

Inside and I don't see her. I dump the bag on the sofa, step into the kitchen, into the bedroom, and she's not there.

And she calls out, 'I'm in the jacks.'

'Right.'

I hear paper rustling so I turn on the TV to save her from the embarrassment she won't have. She calls out to turn it off. She rustles again, flushes, washes, walks out, laptop bag over her shoulder, and I turn off the TV.

'Sit with me,' she says, putting her bag down. She's wearing a blue suit with a too-short skirt, a touch of a dirty Margaret Thatcher about her. 'Sit at the breakfast bar,' she says.

'This your first time in my flat without me being here?'

'None of your fucking business.'

I sit and she finishes making the coffee she had already started.

'Did you see Martin outside?'

'Aye.'

'Did he tell you I was raging?'

'No.'

'Liar,' she says. 'And he's right. I am. Or I was. I've calmed down.'

'I didn't think you were so brittle, Imelda.'

'Not brittle,' she says, 'brittle is easily broken. I think maybe I just don't like weak men working for me.'

And she puts a mug down at my closed hands, takes a stool, takes a drink, tucks some stray hair in behind an ear, looks me in the eye.

'Don't take fucking liberties with our connection,' she says. 'Don't take liberties with your role in all of this. If we don't have a pecking order, we just have a mess, understand? There has to be a pecking order. There always has to be a hierarchy. That's how society works. It's how humans work, how we all get fed. A dog doesn't want a master, *it has to have a master*.'

And this is all a little haywire, all a bit crazy.

'Wait a wee second here,' I say. 'I have no problem with a pecking order. I have a problem with the fact that you could park a convoy of Volvos in the gaps in our security.'

She takes a drink, thinks for a moment, puts the cup back down, goes 'What do you know?'

'I can't say. Not here.'

'You know nothing, in other words.'

'Not true. I've had some feedback from someone. I know for a fact there are people who know things they have no business knowing. Things about me, Imelda. Things about you. Things you said you would stop people from getting to know. I find it a little hard not to mention all of that when everything depends on our work staying in the shadows.

'All that stuff you do, that taking shit for granted, not being bothered about the detail, all that it'll be all right in the morning shite, it's all a bit Irish, isn't it? Lovely and quirky and easy on the ear, but it's got failure written all over it. It's the kind of shite that gets people dead in this line of work. They might think they have no reason in the world to die, but that's what gets them dead.'

And she's looking at me like she's not so interested in anything I'm saying, and she says, 'Where's Martha McStay?'

I go, 'Did you hear what I just said? About security? About your promise being worthless? You think I can ignore this stuff?'

'Where's Martha McStay?'

And she takes another drink of coffee. And I take a drink of mine.

'Let me spell it out, Imelda,' I say. 'We are being listened to and watched and tracked every fucking step of the way. And I mean every step, no matter what you think. Every job. Every name. The name on my fucking passport. You understanding that? We are totally vulnerable, totally compromised, totally at the mercy of anyone who wants to expose or finish us.'

And she goes, 'Answer the fucking question.'

I say, 'Fair enough. Fuck it, fair enough. Where is Martha McStay? Fuck knows. I last saw her on the roof of some truck. She fell ten floors. Why? What did you hear?'

'I heard nothing,' she says. 'I got an off-message call from my asset in the field before the job was supposed to be done and, since then, I have heard nothing. Nada.'

'They haven't found her then?'

'Evidently. You're not bullshitting me, are you?'

'About her falling ten floors?'

'Yes. About her falling ten floors.'

'No, Imelda. I am at this moment confessing to a murder, on tape, in fuck knows how many countries around the world. Probably in Britain, certainly in the US. I am confessing to a murder. Otherwise I'd probably just lie, cover my tracks a bit, but despite being an asset in the field, my chief doesn't want me to cover my tracks. So, yes, I pushed Martha McStay off a fucking roof, she fell, landed on the back of truck. She is dead as fuck.'

'Okay,' she says. 'I got it.'

I get up, shaking my head, walk to the bathroom, put the plug in the bath, turn on the taps, squirt in some bubbles. I walk back to the kitchen and she's watching, curious about my movements.

And I go, 'We were supposed to trust each other Imelda. There is no trust now. We are clowns, all of us, at someone else's circus.'

She nods, finishes her coffee.

I flip open the cupboard above the kettle, take out the only bottle that's in there, an unopened Jameson. I lift down two heavy tumblers and I know she is watching me, curious as a cat. The only sound is the spin of the lid as I open it, lift it off. I pour the whiskey into the glasses and the scent suggests class and craic and caution.

She puts her head to one side as I carry them over, place one in front of her. She clears her throat, maybe taken a little by surprise, looks at the square glass, looks at me.

I hold mine out to clink it. She sighs and decides and I'm holding my hand there. And holding. And holding.

And she gets there, lifts hers, touches mine, we say '*Sláinte*'.

I say, 'And peace.'

She nods.

I say, 'Who is number four?'

'Come again?'

'Who is next on the list?'

And she grins, waves at me, as if saying goodbye.

She goes, 'Wise up.'

'Who is it?'

'I can't tell you that. It's months away. Forget it. Take some time to yourself, Aloysius.'

'Who is it?'

'Forget it.'

And I'm nodding.

She goes, 'Who were you speaking with?'

'What?'

'Who were you speaking with about our operations?'

'No one.'

'Who told you about the gaps in our security.'

'I can't tell you, it's not—'

She goes, 'Exactly. Same.'

And I'm thinking she doesn't even believe me. I'm thinking now she reckons I made that up, that I'm trying to stir the pot, push myself forward, climb the ladder. I reckon she thinks I made it up so that I seemed like a guy with more than she thought I had.

'I'm not lying,' I say, 'about that information. I'm not making it up. Someone could be toying with me, yes, but I've still been told what I said I'd been told.'

She smiles sweetly, patronisingly.

And we pause.

'I had one other question,' I say, 'but I don't want to ask it.'

'You can ask it.'

'I was going to ask you to have a bath with me. I wanted to know if we could share one, chill out, lose a couple of hours. But I don't want to ask you that. You see, I think I've misread you enough. Everything is telling me that I've lost a skill I once had. So I won't ask you to have a bath with me.'

She doesn't bat an eyelid, doesn't look at me or look away, doesn't drum her fingers or say a word.

Uncomfortably enough, she sits back now, looks around her – at the uncleaned bits of my life scattered on the coffee table over by the TV, at the way I left my curtains closed, at the way it looks like I've slept on the sofa more times than a man with a bed ever should.

'My husband killed himself,' she says. 'And I've come to know it was the best thing for him to do. I've come to understand it, to see it from his side.'

And I nod. Unexpected interjection in the conversation, but one that makes sense on its own.

'That doesn't mean he wasn't a selfish cunt,' she says. 'It's his anniversary.'

She raises a glass and we clink again.

'I'm sorry,' I say.

'Don't be.'

'Was he a good husband?'

'He was. Better than most, I think. Men have problems, don't they? Problems with their role in the world, with what it means to be male these days, with their simultaneous need to create and destroy, don't they? But he wasn't like that. He was solid, predictable, dependable. Call it boring if you want, but it was what I liked, what I needed in life. And then he did the most unexpected thing of all.'

'I can get that.'

She drinks some more and says, 'Don't give me any surprises Aloysius, and I'll do the same for you.'

'Okay,' I say, and pour another couple of glasses.

'And I'll go and get naked and sit in your bath and drink whiskey,' she says, 'and you'll wait here, leave me to it.'

'Okay.'

'I might call you if I need my back washed.'

'Okay.'

'Can you read all that okay?'

I shake my head, say, 'I needed some time to myself, to chill out, spread out in the bath. I was going to ask you to leave, but then I thought how fucking might make us both feel better. Looks like now I've lost the bath and the fuck. Another misread on my part.'

'Not necessarily,' and she takes a drink.

And I'm wondering if Martin is still outside, waiting for us to finish our showdown, sitting in his four-by-four as she, unexpectedly, takes a bath.

'Should I . . . ?' I've my thumb pointed towards the door.

'I told him to give us an hour or so,' she says. 'Don't worry about Martin. There's no one on earth you should worry about less than Martin. If ever a man had it all sorted out.'

And I shrug.

'Tell me about Martha McStay. Why her?'

'You don't know?'

'I know fuck all about her, to be honest. What sort of story did her life tell?'

'Usual Northern Ireland misguided patriotism from a family

of hateful wankers,' she says. 'Aged sixteen, beat a paramilitary commander to death when he touched her arse. Locked away for a while, ended up in love with some crazy Polish ex-soldier, ran drugs for him in Belfast, killed him, fucked off east with the cash.'

Imelda rubs at her face, tired of all of this, tired on this day her husband died.

She goes, 'So she came home a couple of years later, helped spring her nutcase dad as he was going to a court hearing. Arranged for an ambush, shot two prison guards in the head. Got completely away with it, by the way, to the point where the mud didn't even get thrown, let alone stick. These days her dad's living somewhere in Ukraine, making all sorts of dodgy connections and showing up at illegal arms fairs. They had been keeping in touch via handwritten letters, full of codes the intelligence lads were never able to break.

'Anyway, Martha was, as you will have gathered, charismatic, sexy, sharp as a tack, and one by one every fucking flag-waving loon was falling at her feet. And her latest move had been to become a politician. She was high-speed becoming the most divisive fucking fool in the North.'

I say, 'So why the hard solve?'

'Why? Because she was sitting on a stockpile of nine tonnes of high explosives and two hundred AK-47s. Because she had thirteen   simultaneous bombings planned for 2022, anniversary of the foundation of the state. Because she was going to be nowhere near any of it when it happened. She was running rings round Irish and British political and security figures and half of them reckoned they were the targets themselves. She had too many people looking over their own shoulders. The truth is that neither the Brits, nor the Yanks nor even any of us on this busy little island had seen anything like the threat that passionate little Martha was starting to pose. She was a fucking red alert, Aloysius, and just getting more and more dangerous. There was nothing on her, nothing legal. There was nothing legitimate anyone could do. And people like that lend themselves well to sudden death. The conspiracy theorists have so little hard data it makes her unworthy. Hence the hard solve.'

I go, 'Jesus.'

'A woman like that could set a country back sixty years. She could cost it more than it could afford. Between the deaths and the emigration and the hatred she was going to cause all of us, she was like the second fucking Famine personified. Some people, you know, are just not necessary.'

'And she couldn't be stopped?'

'Not in any conventional way, no. She knew and loved how much sway she had, knew how to build on it too.'

'Can I see her file?'

'Why?'

'Because I just killed her.'

Imelda nods, takes a drink, says, 'That you did.'

And I'm taking a drink when she says, 'She get to you somehow? She make some kind of impression on you, Aloysius? Before you did the deed?'

I shrug, act it up a bit, look a little coy, say, 'Maybe a wee bit.'

'I'm taking that bath,' she says, stands up, presses two hands in her back, stretches out, turns away.

'Can I see it?'

She stops, 'What?'

'The file.'

'Now?'

'Yes. That okay?'

'Jesus. You in fecking love or something?'

'Please.'

She looks at the laptop in her bag, and back to me.

I say, 'Fifteen hours ago, I let go of her, ten storeys high. She's the only one I hadn't researched, the only one I didn't know all about before I did it, had no clue what she believes in. And, to be honest, it's fucking killing me.'

Imelda pulls her laptop from her bag, opens it on the breakfast bar, keys in a password, brings up a file, sets it in front of me.

'I believe you,' she says. 'But if you do happen to go looking for the fourth name on the list on my laptop, you won't find it.'

I say, 'Maybe better if I don't know it.'

'Yes,' she says. 'You're right about that.' And she's walking to the bathroom as I pull the machine in front of my face.

'You can't go online, by the way,' she says. 'It can't connect to the Internet.'

'No worries,' I say, sliding on glasses as a door closes.

And I shrink the document and scan the desktop. All the files are numbers, weird words, random jumbles of letters. There's some kind of code going on here. I click one open and it's images of a roadside, shots of where the white lines are. I click another and it's police pictures of Danny Latigan floating, dead and bloated, in his own swimming pool.

I click one and see pictures of an airport. One document has a breakdown of government spending on state security. Another lists millions of words, none of them in any language I've seen before.

'Fuck,' I say.

And I hear her getting in, sliding down. I thought she'd have me join her, thought I could have stolen away to rifle her laptop, but this is an even better opportunity.

I click onwards, looking for patterns, for images, for clues as to what might be a live or imminent project. And there's nothing, nothing, nothing.

What am I looking for?

The next on the list. The next on the list.

So I'm looking for the list.

And what do I know about the list?

I know Latigan is on it. I know Marley and McStay are on it.

I hit search and type them all – Latigan, Marley, McStay. There's one document that has all of those in it, called 'data bridge 3994'.

I click through, and we're talking 200,000 words of what looks like total shite. More random words, often repeated dozens of times. Random names, numbers, colours, towns, cities, countries.

But I see Latigan now, I see the word appears nineteen times. And I look at it, flick through all of them, looking at it typed nineteen times.

And I look at them all, at what's around them. But it's all just other names, words, numbers. It goes 'celia yellow park tramlines Latigan charleston dundee shelf 208839 upswing . . . ' and on it goes, bullshit galore.

Yet there, in the tenth mention, perhaps just by luck, I see it's different. The second letter is an italic.

It's all Latigan, then I see L*a*tigan.

An odd little happening.

And in the tenth mention of the word Marley, it's M*a*rley.

And in the tenth mention of McStay, it's M*c*Stay.

'Wow,' I say, chuffed with myself, pleased at the code cracking. This must be something she's shared, something printed, maybe passed to Martin, passed to whoever it is they talk with.

But I have 200,000 words in front of me now and, I realise, I'm looking for a word I don't know that has an italic as a second letter.

'Wow and shite,' I say.

Can I search for italics?

And, I don't know why, but she's getting out of the bath now. Why is she doing that?

I hear her getting out and she goes, 'Aloysius?'

A questioning tone, a word that is a whole question.

Fuck it. So can I search for italics? I can't even google that question. No wait, I can, my phone.

She goes, 'Aloysius?'

Says use 'Find', then 'Advanced Find', then 'Format', then 'Font Style'.

She's drying herself off in there, the shortest bath in history.

She goes, 'Just a little question for you.'

I get it to find all italicised 'A's in the document. It brings up one L*a*tigan, one M*a*rley.

I try '*e*' and there's none.

She goes, 'Aloysius?'

Then '*i*' and there's – no, wait.

The door opens, I can hear the towel being tugged as she tightens her dressing gown.

And there it is. One entry, an answer to my question. Second letter an italic.

I click off the search box.

She is behind me now, reaches over, closes the laptop.

'You not hear me?'

'I did. Thought you were calling me in. I was just going to get the whiskey.'

She goes, 'You said "Not what she believes in".'

'What?'

'You were talking about having killed Martha McStay and you said, quote, that you didn't know "What she believes in".'

'Meaning?'

'Meaning present tense. Meaning, in your mind, she's alive.'

I stand, say, 'Fuck you, Imelda. Not this bullshit again. You're finding trouble where there is none.'

'None?'

'None. You're paranoid.'

'No, not paranoid. Just annoyed.'

'I know how that feels.'

And I wait for a retort, a hard-to-follow comeback, and she's just looking at me, her toes gripping the carpet beneath her. Gripping and releasing. Gripping and releasing.

And I'm thinking how she's the leader of the pack, how she's the top dog, how she's at the top of the pecking order and how I'm throwing myself around too much within it.

She's looking at me, at my face, trying to read it, trying to see what's going on under this big blank front of mine. She's looking at it, all suspicious now, and all she sees is suspicious looking back at her.

And all I can think of is Martin.

He'll be parked up outside now.

Martin's outside.

Martin's outside.

He's next on the list.

Chapter Twenty-three

March 2017

I'VE TOLD Martin I should drive. He hasn't a clue what's happening or where we're going, but we're going fast.

'Trust me,' I say.

'I do,' he says. 'Is Imelda okay?'

'She'll be fine,' I say. 'Trust me.'

We take the tolled tunnel, spitting us out on the top side of Dublin, onto the M1 motorway, heading north, the far side of the speed limit.

He's gripping the assist handle above the door, asks, 'You stressed out or what?'

'Just making progress, Martin. Just moving ahead with things.'

'I've got a 7 PM dinner with a TD in Ballsbridge,' he says. 'I need to be there.'

'You need to be here first,' I say.

We tear on and my brain is racing like the wheels. I won't tell him right now, but I will tell him that I am running from the certainty that Imelda is seeking to have me take his life.

I am running because she knows I have found out what she insisted I must not know, that everything she has told me has been an act of betrayal. I am running before she has set me up with the murder of Martin. I am running in anger.

She wants me to be her hard-fanged puppy, some kind of cruel fool for her, and she believes she can get me to do that? Her patriotism is poison. Her loyalty is piss weak. She is the one who deserves to be thrown off a building.

I saw this coming. I'll say it again, I saw it coming. I die, that's what happens at the end of this story. I die in the moments after I kill Martin.

Maybe armed police catch me in the act, tipped off in some random call, and have been encouraged to shoot. Maybe it'll be some undercover tough that who kills me, who gets lauded for taking out the unknown, homeless fucker who took down one of the nation's best servants.

That's what will happen – you can be sure of it – because then there will only be Imelda, the forever friend of whoever it was in the high place that paid for all of this. Only fucking Imelda and dead men with their secrets.

There is dirt in my throat now, some bits of grit and filth crawling coarsely up from the back of my tongue, and I want to spit, to shout and rage at the fucking world with a mouth full of mud.

★

There's a sprawling service station, a pull-in plaza, and I drop the gears and cruise in, tucking up in the furthest corner of the car park. I reverse into the space, facing the building, the back of the vehicle against a field dotted with cud-chewing cows.

I cut the engine and note that it's busy, that there's dozens of other cars, other four-by-fours, lorries, vans, parents, children. And I'm thinking busy is good, that people and CCTV and daylight are all good because there are two men in this vehicle who are due to be killed, one after the other.

It hits me now, this second, as Martin looks at my face, that I didn't look up my own name on that bloody laptop. I didn't even get to look for a second italic marking me for death, but then maybe such a detail was too dirty even to write.

He goes, 'This what you wanted to show me? A fucking shop?'

I hear myself sigh, maybe a bit of sadness. It's maybe some tiredness and maybe some sliver of relief all mixed into one.

'I wish it was that simple,' I say. 'I had to get out of Dublin. I had to get us both out of Dublin, just until I can get a grip on all of this.'

'Explain,' he says. 'Calm down, Aloysius, and explain.'

And I breathe in deep, look all around. The cows in the mirror looking our way, contented, uncomplicated, unknowing and, therefore, unbothered by their fate.

I see a mum chuckling as she walks her three-year-old by the hand, as the little boy talks excitedly about everything that comes into his head.

'Dangerous days,' I say, turning to him. 'And they didn't have to be. I have some information you need to know.'

He opens his door and the noise makes me jolt.

'Come on,' he says, 'let's chat.'

The air eases around me, nicely, comfortably, as we walk across the car park and into the café.

'I've made mistakes in my life,' I say to him, a hot, paper-cupped coffee in my hand. 'All sorts of shit, stuff that nearly got me killed, some stuff that at times made me want to get killed. Truth is, I sometimes don't trust my thinking. Fact is, I sometimes put too much trust in my gut, sometimes too little. It's all done often without taking full stock of all the circumstances. I don't know if that balancing act keeps me sane or keeps me mad.'

His eyes, wide open yet yellowed and dimmed, take all this in, encourage more of this lid-lifting.

And I go, 'I have to tell you that, all along, I've had doubts about this whole project. Where my head said everything is fine, my gut said it's too easy, said go easy, keep looking over your shoulder, keep looking at Martin, at Imelda.

'You know I'm not what you might call someone who set out to kill or die for his country. Yet you know too that I've been looking for a place, a part to play, some kind of sense of creating some kind of half-sensible life story. So I've been playing the part, Martin. And I've been out in the field hard-solving your problems, Ireland's problems, and it's been working for me. It's been like coming home, but coming home on my terms, coming home as so much more of a human being than I was when I left. But I've kept my eyes open. And now I've got some information on this little organisation of yours, of ours.

'I got to hear, loud and clear, that the Americans know every detail of it, that they're tracking the whole thing, by the day, by the hour. And today I got to learn that Imelda doesn't care about that, or doesn't care enough to even look into it, as if it is all ending, as if the end is already certain and all she wants to do is close the book.

'And today I also got to learn that she won't tell me who's number four on the list. So when we were in my flat, I did a bit of digging.'

He takes a drink, 'And what did you find out?'

I say, 'It's you, Martin,' and his big face is unmoved, the face of the practiced professional, the show of the diplomat who thinks and calculates and plans before he gives anything away.

'At some stage, pretty soon,' I say, 'Imelda is planning to talk me into killing you. She's going to set you up, I think, maybe lead me to believe I am under threat from you, I don't know. But, much as she knows she can talk me into many things, I'm not going to do that. I can't do that. It is a betrayal, cruel and, I think, very unfair, very un-Irish.

'My own name may not be on that list, but you can be sure my fate is as certain as yours, my death will be the direct result of yours, and our two deaths clean this whole thing up very neatly for her, for the government, for whoever it is that funds this show. I need you to believe that Imelda Feather is not on your side, hard as it may be to swallow. She is the opposite, and she is the most dangerous person in this whole thing.'

And I know I haven't even given him a moment to think, to digest this heavy load. All there is now, and it's barely perceptible, is a little smirk, a micro mocking of what I have just said.

He goes, 'How do you know this?'

'The list.'

'That massive document on her laptop?'

'Yes.'

'With one letter in the names in italics?'

'Yes. That's it. You're the fourth name.'

'I am,' he says. 'And I knew that, you big clart.'

'You knew that?'

'Yes,' he goes, and breaks into laughter now. 'Of course I did, fuck's sake, Aloysius, you prick.'

And he's still laughing, waving a hand to let it all clear from his belly, wiping an eye and enjoying it.

I can't help but laugh too, smile and laugh at his reaction.

I say, 'You knew that I'm supposed to kill you?'

'Yes, yes, yes,' he says. 'Fuck's sake, yes, I know all of that.'

'What the fuck, Martin? So you're some kind of mole in this outfit?'

'No, no,' he goes, chuckling again. 'No, for fuck's sake. Jesus Christ, you're getting carried away now. I know you're supposed to kill me and, what's more, I damn well hope you do.'

Martin gets up, goes and buys two brownies, and I watch him all the way, leaner than he has been in a while, beaming happily at the woman behind the counter. He comes back, plops one in front of me.

'Not hungry, thanks,' I say, making a face that says he's doing my head in.

He eats and chuckles again and I watch him.

Martin tells me I wasn't supposed to have received this information for months, that I had broken in and seen something I shouldn't have seen.

'There are no betrayals, Aloysius,' he says. 'There are just complications, things that don't seem to make sense on the surface. It's the kind of business we have all chosen to get into, y'know? You're looking for black and white and the whole thing is multi-coloured.

'I told you from the start that you could trust Imelda with anything, and I meant that. It's truer now than it ever was. She would die before she'd turn her back on you. And she would do the same for me.'

And I'm saying, 'I don't understa—'

'No,' he goes, 'because you're the blunt instrument. You're the hammer head, not the guy deciding if he should swing the thing. There's a structure to all of this, an order. Don't you worry about how that all fits together, we just need each person to do their bit for the operation to run cleanly.'

'Martin,' I say, 'you wanker. You seriously want me to kill you?'

'Look in my eyes, Aloysius. Look at these tired eyes. I'm dying, my friend. I have four to six months before I shuffle off this mortal coil. I am rotten with cancer. I have it all over me like a wet week, bones to bollocks. I was too slow to find out and I'm way too long in the tooth for a massive dose of chemo, and for surgery that has a 5 percent chance of working.

'But I'm living the lives of ten men with what we've been doing. I've never been happier, never prouder, never more ready to die. I've never seen justice like it, I've never seen the whip so fairly cracked in Ireland in my life and, at the back of every mind in the nation, there's a happy little song, even if they don't know where it came from.'

He tells me his own murder is his best way out, and that it must very clearly be a murder. He tells me it's the fastest, cleanest way, that it unlocks a massive insurance bundle for his estranged wife, and for his daughter if she ever comes home. Under his policy, he says, a suicide or death by cancer would never provide as much.

'But you know what the real craic is?' he asks.

'No.'

'The real craic is that if you don't get me first, the Americans or the British will.'

'Kill you?'

'In the end, as good as. But they'll disappear me, it's a certainty. They will take me and interrogate the living fuck out of me, and I can't go through that. I can't face that, can't survive that. They don't know and, the fact is, they wouldn't care that I'm a dying man. They have very serious unfinished business with me and they want to move when we have finished the list, when I've stepped away from you and Imelda into obscurity, living alone, they want to pick me up and take me away.

'They can't do it now because I'm with Imelda every day, regularly in touch with people in high places, but they need to do it soon. I'm told they will move when number four goes down. For me, Aloysius, that would be a fate, literally, worse than death. And that's why I'm number four.'

Walking to the door, heading back to the vehicle, he says, 'When we started this whole thing, me, Imelda, a couple of guys in the civil service, a couple of political people, we started with fuck all. In fact we started with less. As soon as we did anything, they knew. The Yanks, the Brits. They just had so many ears on our phones and software, red-flagging every conversation that they knew of, even if the topic was of no interest to them at all.

'But we couldn't have that. It left us vulnerable. So we turned the tables, succoured them in, started conversations that made us more interesting to them. Mad stuff. Stuff we made up. And when we got them closer, when they felt we really did have a few direct lines into people and places of interest to them, we got to asking them for help. And the help came.

'And, Jesus, it was a hoot. We were spinning fucking tales about the Brits to the Yanks and vice versa. We were filling them with shite about what the hard left were up to, about what all sorts of terrorists are up to. You know the sort of twats that like to wander about Belfast and Dublin in revolutionary T-shirts, hoping to smell blood and talk about bombs? We told the Yanks we knew a load of those guys were setting up a cyber terrorist camp in Athlone. They believed it, too.

'Then when Kiera went off to Iraq – my daughter – our contacts went apeshit with joy, asked me if I thought she could be turned to work for the west and all of that and I said "Oh aye definitely, not a bother", and they formed a whole unit aimed at finding her and getting word to her.'

He holds the door open for me and he's saying, 'Sure I told the posh boys at MI6 there was a secret American base in Galway where they were torturing some Islamic State fellas, for fuck's sake. The whole county had drones flying over it before I was home for dinner.

'At one stage we had them telling themselves the Irish were their best friends. We had them thinking, *Ack sure the Irish chat away and everyone chats away to the Irish and sure maybe the Paddies will be of use to us.* And, by fuck, I filled them with a load of dung, so I did. Never enjoyed myself more, to be honest with you. With even the little bits of feedback I was getting from a few old, good contacts, it wasn't long at all before we knew how they did their listening, where they did it and the sort of stuff they were most interested in. Great craic altogether.'

And we stop walking when I ask, 'And in return?'

'Well, I got a few favours from them. I found out about my daughter, where she is, who she's with, about her health, if there were grandchildren on the way. They got me enough to know she's a lost cause, but that she's found some kind of happiness.

'To be honest, we got all we needed to know about a few dozen people. We couldn't possibly have done all the work ourselves. Wouldn't have had the resources, the manpower, the experience. Basically, we just bluffed the holes off ourselves. It wasn't even too hard. We got to learn things we could never have known. We found out who says what about us around the world, who owes us, who is planning to fuck us in one way or another. We got what we needed, got watching who we wanted and, one day, we stopped pissing around and drew up a little PR plan, a little list.

'And then we went looking for the right man and found out all about you, Aloysius. We got to learn what you've done, where you've been, your deadly wee business on the dark net. Most of it anyway. We evaluated you for a long time before moving in. We knew you were the man for the job.

'But now the curtain is closing and I have a few bills to pay, one way or another. They want to know how much of this and that and the other is true, how much is a load of balls, and they will not be leaving any of us alone until they get what they need, I'm afraid. It was only a matter of time until we were rumbled, and that time is now.

'They want me to know I cost them all millions and learned too much in the process, that I basically stole a pile of their information. They really do not like the fact I had the fucking nerve to do it in the first place, y'know? You talk about this mad thing in your head about Imelda wanting to bump you off because you know too much. You? Fuck's sake, you wouldn't believe what I know about the CIA and MI6 and what they're up to and who's who and what's what. In their world, I have become a very dangerous man.'

And his words are making sense, and a pattern is forming. I can see how the Americans are sitting it out until the coast is clear, I can see how that clearly says they are taking him. I can see why Martin has been so careful to keep his illness such a close, close secret. Clearest of all, I can see how all of what he found was handed to him on a plate by people who are angry they didn't know better. Wounded pride can make nations act in the wildest of ways, nations like the US, like the UK, like Ireland.

And, right on cue, I see now three vehicles I don't like in this car park. I see there are men in all of them, and that all of the men are watching without speaking.

'But,' he says, walking now, 'it's left us with some good smarts, and a good reputation in places where we needed it. We might be the silly little guys to the big guys, Aloysius. But it's like the cat and the lion, just a matter of scale, nothing else. And it's no bad thing when the lion feels he has to keep an eye on the cat from now on because he knows the cat is as smart and sleek and as stout-hearted as he is.

'So, aye, of course they're watching us, watching us like hawks, but they don't know the details of what's ahead, and we do. And, Aloysius, my friend, you have a job to do.'

I'm about to tell him not to say any more when he makes the point.

'You're about to tell me they're here,' he says, stopping now, checking out what he can of my thoughts from my face.

My instinct is to run. To run at them. To run from them. Right now, immediately, fast as hell.

'Take it easy, just walk with me back to the car,' he says.

'They'll take you now, Martin. They know something's changed. I've landed you in this shit and they'll take you now while they can.'

'They will,' he says. 'They'll have had shotgun mikes on us, they'll have heard everything I just said to you, in which case they'll not want the man who's going to kill me to be around for long either.'

We get to the vehicle and I open the passenger door for him, looking back at the cars. I spit on the ground, sending a message, marking my turf as I go to the driver's seat, climb in, close the door, watch.

'They will take me, Aloysius, and they will leave you here,' he says. 'They know who you are and they won't feel the need to do you any favours. You will be stretched across the seat, maybe a drugs overdose. But they will leave you here, dead, unable to tell the story I just told you. You understand?'

'Yes.'

'I cannot live my last days in hostile custody, do you understand?'

'Yes.'

'I want you to take orders from me and I do not want you to bend or breach them in any way, is that clear?'

'Okay,' I say, and I feel the adrenaline fill my limbs, feel the courage scaling up inside, feel how all fear will now be wrapped up and brought along for the ride, be present yet with no active role to play.

'Start the engine,' he says.

And I do.

'Lock the doors.'

I do it.

He goes, 'There's a 9mm and magazine under your seat. Flip open the catch beneath you and you'll find them.'

And the three cars begin to move, fanning out, moving slowly through the lines of other cars as they approach.

He goes, 'Got them?'

'Yes,' I say, and I lock one into the other, hands doing it from memory before I asked them.

'I want you to knock off the safety catch and put it to the centre of the back of my head.'

And he turns, looking out his side window, as the cars close in.

I go, 'Yes,' and place the weapon against the back of his head, the steel against his skull.

The cars speed up. A side door opens, one man ready to leap out, desperate to stop this killing, desperate to get their hands on Martin and bring him in.

Martin goes, 'Did you know what that Kris fella had done before you strung him up and watched him die?'

'What?'

'Did you know about the women-beating and revenge porn? It's always troubled me, always made me wonder about you.'

Karson is out, dashing towards us, one hand waving, one holding a weapon close to his leg.

'I knew,' I say. 'I always know what they've done. I've never killed a good man.'

'Good,' he says. 'Today you will.'

I go, 'Yes.'

He says, 'You will shoot twice.'

I go, 'Yes.'

Karson's panting, one second from Martin's window. Karson, armed and primed, black top and jeans, clean and sober. He looks only at me, pulls on the handle, shakes his head, goes, 'Aloysius, wait, wait.'

Martin says, 'I have no crushing final words or any of that shite, only thank you, trust Imelda and run like fuck.'

Karson, lifts his weapon, points it right at me through the window, other hand still waving, knocking, 'Aloyisus,' he goes, 'don't do this. If you shoot him, I've no choice but . . . '

And as I tilt the weapon and go, 'Thank you, Martin,' I see the reflection of him closing his tired eyes.

The first bullet pushes through flesh, brain and bone, through the window and into Karson's face in one hard, bloody instant. The second bullet does the same, catching the American as he is thumped back, as he drops.

Martin's head has slammed into the glass, fallen back.

As others are getting out, as the three cars surround the front of the vehicle, I toss the gun and hit reverse. The windscreen shatters, scattering fragments into my face, I drop down. The BMW four-by-four punches over the kerb behind, roars up the bank and cracks into the fence. I feel the traction kick in on four corners as we pull further back up into the field, reversing fast towards chewing cattle.

I slam into first as another bullet smashes indoors, hitting the wheel at twelve o'clock.

I grab Martin, pull him upwards, push him into the seated position and it's enough to confuse and draw the fire for the second I need. Martin is hit in the face as I blast forwards, back down the slope, ramming into a shooter who is too late to get out of my wide way. He vanishes under the front as I romp further down, is crushed with a bounce, and now hammering between two of the cars, walloping them from my path, off my ground.

More shots, the side and the back and I'm tearing through the car park, stunned citizens leaping out of the way.

In seconds I'm on the slipway, heading south on the motorway, gunning for Dublin.

One car peels out behind, a red VW Golf, slaloming through a scattering of cars and closing fast.

I chunk up the speed, eighty to one hundred, and the Golf is gaining. Martin is slipping onto the floor, his head at the hand-brake, spilling blood, as I push deeper into the engine.

The machine raises its game without protest, ticks calmly to 120 mph, and the Golf is feeling the pace. But it's still strong in play as we hit 130, as I speed past the cameras, lights flashing.

A long, wide bend and I see a clear stretch, the Golf tenaciously on the trail. The driver hits full beam, something to catch my eye, to show fury, and I know that with time, with lightness and agility, as we swoop in and out of cars in our way, it will reach me.

Closing.

Closing.

Moving in now.

And as they come close behind I tip the wheel right, glancing into the middle, chewing up the white lines, a plane at take-off.

Closing, closing again, and I put on the hazards, seeking distraction, seeking to confuse the picture.

And I see two men inside, not speaking, cold faces. And I see now the driver wears a seatbelt, the passenger does not, fresh back into the car after trying to kill me.

The faintest squeal of a police siren in the background.

I hit the fog lights, feigning braking, and there's barely a blink.

I push flat, flat to the board, and we're moving to 140 mph.

We're flying, zooming, roaring past everything on and around this road.

I check my seatbelt, hold myself steady.

I brace.

I tighten up.

I clear my mind.

I loosen.

I relax.

And I ram the footbrake with all I have –

Silence.

Lightness.

Lights flashing.

A muddle of nice, full emotions.

Conscious that the quiet in my ears is total, that the volumes of the road have rolled away, that no birds are singing underneath.

A flicker on the satnav screen seems to take a long time, happens in slow motion. The 9mm pistol arcs gracefully in front of Martin's face as he turns to me, definitely grinning, definitely spinning blood around the cabin.

And there is the certainty now that something hard is about to happen, and it will happen in something like a split second.

A slap like hard wind, like a tornado now, into my back. Air bag explodes, a face into concrete, seeing flashes, and we spin, spin, spin.

My head hits the window, the back of the chair. Martin's face hits me, one of his legs now, kicks my chin. There's noise, rapid beeping from the dash. Some system frantic and panicked.

I blink hard, breathe in, taste my own blood on my face. Feels like we've stopped moving, or we're about to stop moving. I look at the road, at the scenery, everything jerking into view, falling into place like some shoved jigsaw.

And now the picture has stopped moving.

I flip open the door, seeing double, our vehicle's nose lathed down flat by the crash barrier. We have been rammed and spun by our friend behind, we have been slammed into the steel, we have been skidded along.

I walk, legs shaking, and realise I have the weapon in hand, that I auto-found and auto-took it from among the broken glass and big dead body in that murdered vehicle.

There is some of a man in the middle of the road, limbs ripped, clothes, skin torn off, a long thick trail of blood telling me hit the tarmac fifty feet before he stopped moving.

The Golf has no nose, no glass, has rolled, is back on all fours, engine revved to the max and pulling itself apart, all lights flashing like a jackpot.

The driver is intact, airbagged, eyes closed, nose bleeding. The siren wail is rising in volume, cars pulling to a stop three-hundred yards behind.

He opens his eyes, his world spinning. He looks, tries to figure out who, what or why. Or anything. But nothing is working for him.

I raise the weapon and shoot him twice through the side of the head.

Now my legs are trying to take me somewhere, trying to walk me or run me in some direction, for some reason, for some purpose I can't think through.

And it's all just turning upside down and I thought I had the weapon in my hand but I don't and I don't know.

Chapter Twenty-four

March 2017

I'M STRETCHING out my back, arching it, pulling on muscles all bunched together. I do the same with my legs, pointing and pushing my toes, realigning myself, slowly regrouping, reloading, and I open my eyes.

Imelda Feather's head has flopped back into the corner of the armchair, one of those chairs for the elderly, one of those with the high, straight backs that feel so good to sit against. Her mouth is a little open as she snores gently.

It's a hospital bed I'm in, a curtain all around us, the walking and low chatter of relatives and friends beyond. I'm wearing new pyjamas, a new dressing gown folded up on my bedside table.

'Hey,' I say, and she's out cold. I rub at my face, feel a jab of pain from my lower back, see I've got a tag around my right wrist.

I strain my eyes and realise I've got a little headache, a gentle, delicate hurt that I don't want to annoy in case it gets worse.

The tag reads 'Marcus Tempo.'

'Hey,' I say, louder now, and she's not for moving, only for breathing in deep, only for dozing hard.

I watch her and think of Martin, her friend, our friend, shot in the head. And there's something sad about her now, crunched up in that old woman's seat, lonelier and lonelier as the days click by, as the pillars of her life get knocked over one by one.

But I can't think of this. I need information.

I look around my bed. She's left a newspaper further down and I pull up a leg, slide it towards me, grab the pages. I fuck the news-paper at her and she jolts in her seat.

'Jesus,' she goes.

'Wake up.'

'Fuck,' she goes, 'how long was I out?'

'No idea. I just woke up. What time is it?'

She looks to her watch, pulls her head back to allow her eyes to read it.

'9:14,' she says, 'and that's morning time.'

I go, 'Christ.'

'Indeed,' she says, sitting up, waking up.

'What's the story?'

'What do you remember?'

'Everything up to the crash. My back hurts. Head and back.'

'You were hit pretty bad,' she says.

'Cops?'

She shakes her head and I nod.

And she shakes it again and the eye contact says it, the words too heavy to bring forward just now, too risky in case they make a mood that gets in the way of the next thing that must be done.

She's thinking his name, Martin, and I'm doing it too. She

knows I killed him. She knows I had to. She has the strangest form of anger written into her half-slept skin.

'First thing's first,' she says. 'So listen to me, okay? Full attention.'

'Okay.'

'There was a drug deal, a handover, a couple of million worth, going on at that garage yesterday.'

'Okay.'

'Russians and Romanians, okay?'

'Right.'

'It went tits up. Someone tried to pull a fast one with the cash. Guns came out. Martin was getting into his car and one of them ran for him, to get his vehicle, to escape. They killed him, stole it, rammed into the others, took off down the motorway.'

'Right.'

'Bit of a smash a few miles down the road. Another bit of a shoot up. A couple of other cars, innocent people caught up in all of that.'

'Right.'

'You were one of them. The guards know the whole story. They know you're doing a bit of undercover work with the government, that you have nothing to do with this. You're cleared to go. You'll never hear of this again, okay?'

'Jesus,' I say. 'Good work Imelda. What about the Americans?'

'They're helping us clean it up. The whole thing is too embarrassing for them. They're telling their own people that a few of their guys went rogue, got pissed in Ireland, some shite like that. They can't be dragged into this. Exposing aggressive US undercover work in Ireland would be a hammer blow to the CIA, even the president, and the Yanks will do anything to avoid that. Between us, we're sorting out a couple of Ruskies and

Romanian guys who will take some of the rap. They'll confess to owning that 9mm you masterfully flung over the road, say that one of the dead guys did the shooting, all do a spell, get transferred, get out, get well paid. It's a dirty deal but it's a deal all the same, been done before. The Americans have a list of names for these sorts of occasions. And it means this thing ends here. Forevermore, no US bodies can in any way be linked to what happened here, understand?'

'Understood,' I say. 'I don't remember throwing the gun over the road.'

'You threw it onto the back of a lorry on the other side of the carriageway. Your plan to hide it, I'd guess,' she says. 'Mustn't have worked.'

'No. It went off when it landed. Driver pulled over, retrieved it.'

'My prints . . . '

'Don't worry,' she says. 'Trust me, okay?'

'Yeah,' I say, 'okay.'

'Martin's funeral is tomorrow morning,' she says, 'and you will not be able to go.'

'Understood.'

'Now stop being a fucking prick because you are creating problems we do not need to have,' she says.

'Yes,' I say.

'And don't ever insult me by not trusting me again, okay?'

'Okay.'

'And if you ever try to lock me in your bathroom again, I will hit you ten times as hard as I already did with that laptop.'

'Sorry.'

'Wanker.'

'You near knocked me out, Imelda. I was either going to have to knock you out or run, and I couldn't knock you out.'

She goes, 'I'd like to see you try and knock me out, you prick.'

I go, 'Right.'

'Now get the fuck up,' she says. 'We're getting out of here.'

And as I go to move, my back fires pain through me, my neck too, way more serious than I thought.

'Get up, you big girl's blouse,' she says. 'You can rest at your flat for a few days. I've a pile of pills for you.'

★

The pain is searing every bone in my body now. Every bone, tooth, hair. Pain in every vain, in every organ. My heart feels exhausted, as if it might just give up. My whole engine is knackered, like I've run a hundred miles, like I've blown up a hundred balloons. It's all maximum fucked by the time I get out of her car and stagger my way, leaning heavy on her, up the steps and into the flat.

I fall on the bed going, 'Jesus Christ, get me some of those pills.'

The high speed motorway shove, the inhuman jolt, has made me feel my age. My mind wants to move ahead, my body needs me to hang back. I'm learning that it isn't always mind over matter, that as the matter wears out it gets only more significant to the mind.

She brings me a cup of tea as I'm stretching myself, spreading out in my fresh bed, seeking an optimum position of comfort.

Imelda sets it down.

Then a hand, hard, slapping me on the face. Again, on the nose.

'What the *fuck*?'

'Where's Martha McStay?'

A punch in the gut.

The agony is unreal.

'Imelda—'

'Where is Martha McStay? No one fell off any fucking roof in Belfast.'

And another sting on the face, the full hard palm of her hand.

'Stop it,' I say, my hands up to protect me. 'I'll tell you.'

She stands there, watching me, intently, fresh fury written all over her.

'She's being held,' I say, 'she can't escape. One call and she's dead, okay?'

'Held? Who the fuck is holding her?'

'I can't tell you. She's as good as dead, okay?'

Slap.

'Fuck you, I can't tell you.'

'Where is she been held?'

'Dublin. It's safe, Imelda. I had to do it that way.'

'Explain.'

'I'd lost faith in you. You ordered it over the fucking phone. I knew we were being listened to. Her being alive was my security in case I got arrested, okay? I couldn't work out if you were on the level or not.'

Slap.

'Fuck off.'

'Where is she?'

'I can't tell you.'

'Who has her?'

'I can't tell you.'

'Then you're in for a bad time.'

'Yeah,' I say. 'It mightn't look like it, but I can handle a bad back and a few digs, Imelda. Belt away, I'm saying fuck all.'

She watches me, takes stock. She goes into the kitchen, gets her bag, returns, gives me my phone.

'Do it,' she says. 'Finish the job.'

'Get out,' I say. 'Leave me the pills, go away, come back tonight. It'll be done and I'll have proof. You don't need to know any more.'

She pulls some hair behind her ears, mulls this over. She pulls pills from the bag, throws them onto the side table beside the tea.

'Do it,' she says. 'Do it and your job is complete and I'll help you get away and do whatever it is you're going to do next in your life.'

'Okay,' I say, 'thank you.'

'Don't fuck me around again,' she says, going for the bedroom door. She pulls it open, stops, says, 'Who was it who said you were being watched?'

'An American,' I say. 'One I met in Amsterdam.'

Imelda nods, 'The one who was shagging your transsexual friend?'

'Yes,' I say, 'Karson.'

'He's CIA,' she says. 'Sent to get close to you a while ago, after they began doubting what Martin was telling them. He'll have been trying to recruit you, find out what was going on.'

'You think?'

'Yes,' she says. 'He will have seized the moment, laid a trust bomb, made you feel like he was only about the truth, while discrediting me. As you might understand, Aloysius, I know how that works. He will have met you again sooner or later.'

I say, 'He did meet me again, Imelda, at the service station.'

'And did you kill him?'

'Yes.'

'Good. The Americans are brushing it up. Go to sleep. I'll see you later.'

She closes the door, arms the alarm, exits the flat. I take stock, of myself, of my room. She has neatly laid out new clothes on a chair, new socks, underwear, jeans, T-shirts, sweaters. There are new shoes underneath. It's a seat waiting for a man. And I see now a new grey suit wrapped in cellophane, and four new shirts hanging from the otherwise-empty rail at the side of the room, more shoes below it.

I go, 'Jesus.'

I check the phone. Twenty-one missed calls from Tall Marianne. Text messages saying 'Call me,' over and over and over again.

Shit.

I take some painkillers, sink them with the tea.

Shit.

Tall Marianne answers, I go, 'You okay?'

She says, 'No. You know anything about Karson?'

And I do, I know what she needs to know about him, that I shot him twice in the face with the same bullets that killed Martin. But none of this can ever be known, never will be known. I have to lie to her now, lie thoroughly, completely, forever, and I hate it.

'No,' I say.

'He went to Ireland,' she says. 'He said he would look you up, but he's vanished.'

'Never heard from him. When was this?'

'Suddenly. Two days ago. Some university thing.'

'Sorry,' I say. And I want to tell her that maybe he's gone for good, that maybe this is his way of dumping her, but I reckon I'll leave that conversation for another call. 'I'll ask around,' I say.

And she's quiet. I can hear she's about to cry – a love lost.

'That fucker,' she says.

'I'll ask around,' I say it again, 'and get back to you.'

'Please do,' she says, and ends the call.

I flick down for Wayne's number, tired now, sore and emotional and with a lot of thinking to do, a lot of resting and thinking and I'm looking forward to it.

I call him and there's no answer. He has her, Martha McStay, in a rented house in Drumcondra. Imelda could never know that Wayne has helped me, that he understood how things had all gone crazy and confused for me, that he was a kindred lost, hard soul. Imelda had threatened to sack him for allowing me to get the better of him, only she knew I would fight her on it. She told Wayne to take some time out, and I hired him in the gap.

I had brought Martha McStay to Dublin, called him on the way. He bunged some landlord some cash, secured the property where I dropped them off together.

'Don't talk to her,' I had told him. 'She's fucking clever. Just keep her invisible. I'll be back either to kill her or free her. It all depends on how this shit with Imelda goes.'

And he said, 'No problem.'

A man like that needs no instructions on how to keep a prisoner, on how to keep one immobile and quiet.

Wayne's phone rings out again for the second time, but he will know I've been looking for him. I need him to know that I will be coming round to kill her as soon as I can.

I feel the pills, heavy doses of Tramadol, already beginning to work, to soothe and sing to all those back muscles, and I stretch again, feel my mind starting to lie down, to talk slower to me, to talk lower.

I'm thinking of where all this will go, if I will get out as cleanly as Imelda thinks I will. I think how even if I do, I turn forty-one next week and I still haven't found anything that looks like any kind of career path.

My mind sliding from grip now and I'm thinking back on those insane secret days of Operation Dante in Israel and Gaza, and tell myself I am programmed not to let those memories in.

I'm thinking now about my father, or the man who killed my father, about him stretching and swimming, holding his breath and hiding from the world, living away from the fact of what he left behind. And I'm thinking now of Martin's daughter Kiera, lost to religion, to the furthest, hardest extremes of superstition in the caliphate.

I wonder if it is right to do the right thing, to want to steal someone away from a life of insidious, bloody myth, to barge into someone's life and feel you're the proof of something, to even just go there to die for rightness, to even just be clear, 3-D-right, for once in a lifetime, about your actions.

I close my eyes and hope for the best for her, for him, for me, for everyone in this world.

Chapter Twenty-five

March 2017

BEEP.

And I can only grin at my old audible friends kicking off, bringing me to life each morning, the old Amsterdam car horns.

I can't say I've missed them, the beeps, the double beeps, the long and short beeps, the little flashes of bad words they sparked from me, the curses in my head they covered like censors.

Beep.

Hello, morning. Hello, Holland. Hello, cars. Hello beeps.

But.

No stars above me now.

And I know it now, these are not car horns.

This is not my old jar of a flat.

This is not Amsterdam.

And I let my eyes fill with this bright room, this Dublin bedroom.

Nothing has changed since I lay down to rest.

I look at my phone, reach for it, and there's nothing, no alerts, no contacts.

Beep.

And the phone rings now, just as I'm leaning to put it back on the table.

I see it's Wayne, looking for me, for information on what to do with a troublesome woman called Martha McStay. And it's a Facetime call, it's Wayne seeking to see me, or Wayne wanting me to see her.

I accept.

Beep.

I go, 'Wayne,' looking at my screen.

And it's only his face, his eyes half open, as if half asleep.

'You all right?'

It looks like the phone is moving away from him, as if he is stretching his arm out. I see above his head now, further into whatever room he is in.

And it's a room I know. It's my room. It's my kitchen. And the positioning is all wrong, the place where his head is, it's too low.

The phone is moving still further back.

It's showing me that Wayne is on the breakfast bar. Correction – it's showing me that Wayne's head is on the breakfast bar, blood fanning out around the base, around where his neck had been.

Beep.

And someone is walking backwards, walking away from Wayne. Someone is leaving what's left of him right there as they come my way.

And they have broken in, cracked their way in through the door, the warning alarm beeping, signalling that the intruder siren will sound in 120 seconds.

I put the phone down and look around, look for something to

help me. I have half a cup of cold tea. That phone and that cup. I try to climb out of bed but my back is hell. And the door clicks, opens, and I'm not even halfway up.

A pistol points right at me, a tall, wide man, at its other end.

Beep.

Behind him, walking backwards, carrying what's left of Wayne, comes Martha McStay, her shoes red with blood. Still in her yoga pants, still with an arse that could catch your eye no matter who, what, why, where, when – no matter if you're about to die.

'Ah. Bollocks,' I say, nowhere to go, run out of road.

There's another guy, walking after her. I know them, both of these guys. Her burly Belfast bodyguards, her loyal to-the-death servants.

Beep.

Martha turns, hands the phone to her armed friend. She looks healthy, unblemished, someone who has not been through any recent, local difficulties at all.

'You know, Aloysius,' she says, taking the pistol off the man, looking it over, pointing it now at me, 'you had no right to come barging into my life.'

Beep.

And I sit back, my back springing a shock through my system, and I'm thinking how, in a matter of seconds, I may never need to ever worry about this back again.

She goes, 'You're not the first person to try to get the better of me, and you really won't be the last.'

I say, 'You are only alive because of me. Think of it that way.'

'No,' she says. 'I am only alive because you couldn't kill me. What was it? Did you take pity? Did you like my intriguing chat? My yoga arse?'

Beep.

I shrug and it hurts, and I feel like a failure and she knows it. My job is the only job in the world where people you should have killed will throw it back in your face.

She says, 'Your friend with the wandering hands has nothing to put his clothes on because of you.'

'What happened?'

'I happened,' she says. 'I elbowed him in the bollocks, then kicked him in the bollocks, then bit him in the bollocks.'

'Right.'

'And then I head-butted him, knocked him back against a wall, knocked him out.'

'Right.'

Beep.

'By the time these two arrived from Belfast,' she says, nodding at each of her bodyguards, 'I had kicked him in the bollocks 317 times, according to my pedometer.'

'Right.'

'Then I cut his noggin off with an electric carving knife, just to be sure.'

'So I see.'

'I have blood all over my good Nikes.'

'I see that too.'

'I'd do the same to you only I haven't time and my foot hurts like fuck.'

I go, 'Right.'

And she's walking closer, that pistol very much looking like it is going to be used according to instructions the manufacturer will not have supplied.

Martha McStay places the barrel on my forehead and I feel how the steel is warm, how it's a weapon that was recently pulled from a jacket, from under a belt.

'And what now?' I say.

Beep.

'Now your number's up, Aloysius.'

And I don't know where it comes from but my mouth says, 'Don't.'

'Why not?'

But I can think of no reason, no honest defence for myself, for my life, no argument against it coming to a close. And I am now not at all annoyed with Martha McStay, not at all angry.

I was thinking about closing my eyes for this, but now I know I'll keep them open.

She goes, 'You should've killed me when you had the chance. Basically, you failed.'

I look up at her dark, lovely, wide eyes, smile my best smile and say, 'Failure is beautiful.'

She goes, 'Yes,' and nods. Goes, 'Yes.'

And I see her thin, hard hand move.

Should Aloysius return?
Speak your mind @LibertiesPress